I0634389

Numismatic and Antiquarian Society of Philadelphia

Proceedings of the Numismatic and Antiquarian Society

Of Philadelphia for the Years 1892-1898

Numismatic and Antiquarian Society of Philadelphia

Proceedings of the Numismatic and Antiquarian Society
Of Philadelphia for the Years 1892-1898

ISBN/EAN: 9783741189593

Manufactured in Europe, USA, Canada, Australia, Japa

Cover: Foto ©Andreas Hilbeck / pixelio.de

Manufactured and distributed by brebook publishing software
(www.brebook.com)

Numismatic and Antiquarian Society of Philadelphia

Proceedings of the Numismatic and Antiquarian Society

PROCEEDINGS

OF THE

Numismatic and Antiquarian Society

OF PHILADELPHIA

FOR THE YEARS 1892-1898

PHILADELPHIA
PUBLISHED BY THE SOCIETY
1899

Numismatic and Antiquarian Society

OF PHILADELPHIA

FOR THE YEARS 1892-1898

PHILADELPHIA

PUBLISHED BY THE SOCIETY

1899

Franklin Printing Company·
PHILADELPHIA

PRINCIPAL CONTENTS.

3

1892.

OFFICERS.

PRESIDENT

DANIEL G. BRINTON, M. D.

VICE-PRESIDENTS.

EDWIN W. LEHMAN,   J. SERGEANT PRICE,
JOHN R. BAKER,   REV. JOSEPH F. GARRISON
W. S. W. RUSCHENBERGER,   LEWIS A. SCOTT,
FRANCIS JORDAN, JR.

HONORARY VICE-PRESIDENTS.

HON. ROBERT C. WINTHROP,   Massachusetts.
HON. AMOS PERRY, ...   Rhode Island.
HON. J. HAMMOND TRUMBULL,   Connecticut.
GEN. J. WATTS DE PEYSTER   New York.
HON. THOMAS F. BAYARD, . .   Delaware.
HON. JOHN H. B. LATROBE,   Maryland.
PROF. G. BROWN GOODE,   District of Columbia.
R. ALONZO BROCK, ESQ., . .   Virginia.
CHARLES C. JONES, JR., ESQ.,   . Georgia.
JOSEPH JONES, M. D., ...   Louisiana.
PROF. JAMES D. BUTLER, ...   Wisconsin.
RT. REV. WILLIAM STEVENS PERRY,   Iowa.
RT. REV. WILLIAM INGRAHAM KIP,   California.

Corresponding Secretary   . BENJ. SMITH LYMAN
Recording Secretary,   . STEWART CULIN
Treasurer, ... THOMAS HOCKLEY
Historiographer . . .   . ELI KIRK PRICE.
Curator of Numismatics,   . FREDERICK D. LANGENHEIM.
Curator of Antiquities,   . CARL EDELHEIM.
Librarian,   . INMAN HORNER.

COMMITTEES.

COMMITTEE ON NUMISMATICS.   COMMITTEE ON ANTIQUITIES.
FREDERICK D. LANGENHEIM,   CLARENCE S. BEMENT,
J. COLVIN RANDALL,   BENJAMIN SMITH LYMAN,
HARRY ROGERS   MAXWELL SOMMERVILLE.

COMMITTEE ON GENEALOGY.   COMMITTEE ON FINANCE.
JOSEPH H. COATES,   J. SERGEANT PRICE,
G. ALBERT LEWIS,   HENRY HÜNGERICH,
ELI K. PRICE.   WILLIAM LONGSTRETH

COMMITTEE ON LIBRARY   COMMITTEE ON HALL.
JOHN M. SCOTT,   THOMAS HOCKLEY,
DAVID MILNE,   B. V. MEIN,
CARL EDELHEIM.   FRANCIS JORDAN, JR.

COMMITTEE ON PUBLICATION.
STEWART CULIN,   REV. JOSEPH F. GARRISON,
BENJAMIN SMITH LYMAN

Hall of the Society, Southeast corner Twenty-First and Pine Sts.

5

1893.

OFFICERS.

PRESIDENT.

DANIEL G. BRINTON, M. D.

VICE-PRESIDENTS.

EDWIN W. LEHMAN,   J. SERGEANT PRICE,
JOHN R. BAKER,   REV. JOSEPH F. GARRISON,
W. S. W. RUSCHENBERGER,   LEWIS A. SCOTT,
             FRANCIS JORDAN, JR.

HONORARY VICE-PRESIDENTS.

HON. ROBERT C. WINTHROP, ... Massachusetts.
HON. AMOS PERRY, ... Rhode Island.
HON. J. HAMMOND TRUMBULL, ... Connecticut.
GEN. J. WATTS DE PEYSTER, ... New York.
HON. THOMAS F. BAYARD, ... Delaware.
PROF. G. BROWN GOODE, ... District of Columbia.
R. ALONZO BROCK, ESQ., ... Virginia.
CHARLES C. JONES, JR., ESQ., ... Georgia.
JOSEPH JONES, M. D., ... Louisiana.
PROF. JAMES D. BUTLER, ... Wisconsin.
RT. REV. WILLIAM STEVENS PERRY, . . . Iowa.
RT. REV. WILLIAM INGRAHAM KIP, ... California.

Corresponding Secretary,   . BENJ. SMITH LYMAN.
Recording Secretary, ... STEWART CULIN.
Treasurer, ... HARRY ROGERS.
Historiographer, ... ELI KIRK PRICE.
Curator of Numismatics, . . FREDERICK D. LANGENHEIM.
Librarian, ... INMAN HORNER.

COMMITTEES.

COMMITTEE ON NUMISMATICS.

FREDERICK D. LANGENHEIM,
J. COLVIN RANDALL,
HARRY ROGERS.

COMMITTEE ON ANTIQUITIES.

CLARENCE S. BEMENT,
BENJ. SMITH LYMAN,
MAXWELL SOMMERVILLE.

COMMITTEE ON GENEALOGY.

JOSEPH H. COATES,
G. ALBERT LEWIS,
ELI K. PRICE.

COMMITTEE ON FINANCE.

J. SERGEANT PRICE,
HENRY JÜNGERICH,
WILLIAM LONGSTRETH.

COMMITTEE ON LIBRARY.

JOHN M SCOTT,
DAVID MILNE,
CARL EDELHEIM.

COMMITTEE ON HALL.

B. V. MEIN,
FRANCIS JORDAN, JR.

COMMITTEE ON PUBLICATION.

STEWART CULIN,   BENJAMIN SMITH LYMAN.

Hall of the Society, Southeast corner Twenty-first and Pine Sts.

6

1894.

OFFICERS.

PRESIDENT.
DANIEL G. BRINTON, M. D.

VICE-PRESIDENTS.

EDWIN W. LEHMAN,
MAXWELL SOMMERVILLE,
W. S. W. RUSCHENBERGER,
J. SERGEANT PRICE,
ROBERT H. LAMBORN,
LEWIS A. SCOTT,

FRANCIS JORDAN, JR.

HONORARY VICE-PRESIDENTS.

HON. ROBERT C. WINTHROP, ... Massachusetts.
HON. AMOS PERRY, ... Rhode Island.
HON. J. HAMMOND TRUMBULL, ... Connecticut.
GEN. J. WATTS DE PEYSTER, . New York.
HON. THOMAS F. BAYARD, . . Delaware.
PROF. G. BROWN GOODE, . . . District of Columbia.
R. ALONZO BROCK, ESQ., . . Virginia.
JOSEPH JONES, M. D., ... Louisiana.
PROF. JAMES D. BUTLER, ... Wisconsin.
RT. REV. WM. STEVENS PERRY, ... Iowa.

Corresponding Secretary,   BENJ. SMITH LYMAN.
Recording Secretary, .   STEWART CULIN.
Treasurer,   HARRY ROGERS.
Historiographer, . . .   JOHN T. MORRIS.
Curator of Numismatics, . . . FREDERICK D. LANGENHEIM
Curator of Antiquities, . B. N. BAILEY.
Librarian, ... CHARLES D. CLARK.

COMMITTEES.

COMMITTEE ON NUMISMATICS.
FREDERICK D. LANGENHEIM,
J. COLVIN RANDALL,
HARRY ROGERS.

COMMITTEE ON ANTIQUITIES.
CLARENCE S. BEMENT
BENJ. SMITH LYMAN,
CORNELIUS STEVENSON

COMMITTEE ON GENEALOGY.
WESTCOTT BAILEY,
G. ALBERT LEWIS,
ELI K. PRICE.

COMMITTEE ON FINANCE.
J. SERGEANT PRICE,
HENRY IUNGERICH,
WILLIAM LONGSTRETH.

COMMITTEE ON LIBRARY.
JOHN M. SCOTT,
DAVID MILNE,
CARL EDELHEIM

COMMITTEE ON HALL.
FRANKLIN PLATT,
B. V. MEIN,
FRANCIS JORDAN, JR.

COMMITTEE ON PUBLICATION.
STEWART CULIN,   BENJ. SMITH LYMAN,
MAXWELL SOMMERVILLE.

Hall of the Society, Northwest corner Broad and Pine Sts.

7

1895.

OFFICERS.

PRESIDENT.

DANIEL G. BRINTON, M. D.

VICE-PRESIDENTS. '

EDWIN W. LEHMAN,   J. SERGEANT PRICE,
MAXWELL SOMMERVILLE,   ROBERT H. LAMBORN,
W. S. W. RUSCHENBERGER.   LEWIS A. SCOTT,

FRANCIS JORDAN, JR.

HONORARY VICE-PRESIDENTS.

PROF. F. W. PUTNAM, ...	Massachusetts.
HON. AMOS PERRY, ...	Rhode Island
HON. J. HAMMOND TRUMBULL,	Connecticut.
GEN. J. WATTS DE PEYSTER, .	. New York.
HON. THOMAS F. BAYARD,	. Delaware.
PROF. G. BROWN GOODE,	. District of Columbia.
R. ALONZO BROCK, ESQ., . . .	. Virginia.
JOSEPH JONES, M. D., . . .	. Louisiana.
PROF. JAMES D. BUTLER, ...	. . . . Wisconsin.
RT. REV. WM. STEVENS PERRY,	. . . . Iowa.

Corresponding Secretary,	BENJ. SMITH LEHMAN.
Recording Secretary, .	. STEWART CULIN.
Treasurer, ...	. . . . HARRY ROGERS.
Historiographer, . . .	. . JOHN T. MORRIS.
Curator of Numismatics,	. FREDERICK D. LANGENHEIM
Curator of Antiquities,	. . B. N. BAILEY.
Librarian, . .	. CHARLES D. CLARK.

COMMITTEES.

COMMITTEE ON NUMISMATICS.
FREDERICK D. LANGENHEIM,
J. COLVIN RANDALL,
HARRY ROGERS.

COMMITTEE ON ANTIQUITIES.
CLARENCE S. BEMENT,
BENJ. SMITH LYMAN,
CORNELIUS STEVENSON

COMMITTEE ON GENEALOGY.
WESTCOTT BAILEY,
G. ALBERT LEWIS,
ELI K. PRICE.

COMMITTEE ON FINANCE.
J. SERGEANT PRICE,
HENRY IUNGERICH,
WILLIAM LONGSTRETH

COMMITTEE ON LIBRARY,
JOHN M. SCOTT,
DAVID MILNE,
CARL EDELHEIM

COMMITTEE ON HALL.
FRANKLIN PLATT,
B. V. MEIN,
FRANCIS JORDAN, JR.

COMMITTEE ON PUBLICATION.
STEWART CULIN,   BENJ. SMITH LYMAN,
MAXWELL SOMMERVILLE.

Hall of the Society, Northwest corner Broad and Pine Sts.

1896.

OFFICERS.

—   ···   -

PRESIDENT
DANIEL G. BRINTON, M. D.

VICE-PRESIDENTS.

J. SERGEANT PRICE,   FRANCIS JORDAN, JR.,
LEWIS A. SCOTT,   MAXWELL SOMMERVILLE.

HONORARY VICE-PRESIDENTS.

PROF. F. W. PUTNAM, ... Massachusetts.
HON. AMOS PERRY, ... Rhode Island.
HON. J. HAMMOND TRUMBULL,   Connecticut.
GEN. J. WATTS DE PEYSTER, ... New York.
HON. THOMAS F. BAYARD, ... Delaware.
PROF. G. BROWN GOODE, ... District of Columbia.
R. ALONZO BROCK, ESQ., ... Virginia.
JOSEPH JONES, M. D., ... Louisiana.
PROF. JAMES D. BUTLER, ... Wisconsin.
RT. REV. WM. STEVENS PERRY. . . . . Iowa.

Corresponding Secretary,   . . BENJ. SMITH LYMAN.
Recording Secretary, ... STEWART CULIN.
Treasurer, ... HARRY ROGERS.
Historiographer, ... JOHN T. MORRIS.
Curator of Numismatics, ... F. D. LANGENHEIM.
Curator of Antiquities, ... B. N. BAILEY.
Librarian,   . CHARLES D. CLARK.

COMMITTEES.

COMMITTEE ON NUMISMATICS.   COMMITTEE ON ANTIQUITIES.
  F. D. LANGENHEIM,   CLARENCE S. BEMENT,
  J. COLVIN RANDALL,   BENJ. SMITH LYMAN,
  HARRY ROGERS.   CORNELIUS STEVENSON

COMMITTEE ON GENEALOGY.   COMMITTEE ON FINANCE.
  WESTCOTT BAILEY,   J. SERGEANT PRICE,
  G. ALBERT LEWIS,   HENRY IUNGERICH,
  ELI K. PRICE.   WILLIAM LONGSTRETH.

COMMITTEE ON LIBRARY.   COMMITTEE ON HALL.
  JOHN M. SCOTT,   FRANKLIN PLATT,
  DAVID MILNE,   B. V. MEIN,
  CARL EDELHEIM.   FRANCIS JORDAN, JR.

COMMITTEE ON PUBLICATION.
STEWART CULIN,   BENJ. SMITH LYMAN,
        MAXWELL SOMMERVILLE.

—   --   -

Hall of the Society, Northwest corner Broad and Pine Sts.

9

OFFICERS.

PRESIDENT.

DANIEL G. BRINTON, M. D.

VICE-PRESIDENTS.

J. SERGEANT PRICE,	MAXWELL SOMMERVILLE,
FRANCIS JORDAN, JR.,	CORNELIUS STEVENSON

HONORARY VICE-PRESIDENTS.

PROF. F. W. PUTNAM,	Massachusetts.
HON. AMOS PERRY, ...	. . Rhode Island.
HON. J. HAMMOND TRUMBULL,	Connecticut.
GEN. J. WATTS DE PEYSTER, . .	New York.
HON. THOMAS F. BAYARD,	. Delaware.
HON. R. ALONZO BROCK,	. . . . Virginia.
PROF. JAMES D. BUTLER, ...	. . . . . . Wisconsin.
RT. REV. WM. STEVENS PERRY,	. . . . Iowa.

Corresponding Secretary,	BENJ. SMITH LYMAN.
Recording Secretary, . . .	STEWART CULIN.
Treasurer, ...	. . . HARRY ROGERS.
Historiographer, ...	. . . . . . JOHN T. MORRIS.
Curator of Numismatics,	. . . . F. D. LANGENHEIM.
Curator of Antiquities.	. B. N. BAILEY.
Librarian, ...	. CHARLES D. CLARK.

COMMITTEES.

COMMITTEE ON NUMISMATICS.

F. D. LANGENHEIM,
J. COLVIN RANDALL,
HARRY ROGERS.

COMMITTEE ON ANTIQUITIES.

WESTCOTT BAILEY,
BENJ. SMITH LYMAN,
CORNELIUS STEVENSON

COMMITTEE ON GENEALOGY.

WESTCOTT BAILEY,
G. ALBERT LEWIS,
ELI K. PRICE.

COMMITTEE ON FINANCE.

J. SERGEANT PRICE,
HENRY IÜNGERICH,
WILLIAM LONGSTRETH.

COMMITTEE ON LIBRARY.

JOHN M. SCOTT,
DAVID MILNE,
CARL EDELHEIM.

COMMITTEE ON HALL.

FRANKLIN PLATT,
B. V. MEIN,
FRANCIS JORDAN, JR.

COMMITTEE ON PUBLICATION.

STEWART CULIN,   BENJ SMITH LYMAN,
MAXWELL SOMMERVILLE

Hall of the Society, Northwest corner Broad and Pine Sts.

1898.

OFFICERS.

PRESIDENT

DANIEL G. BRINTON, M. D.

VICE-PRESIDENTS.

FRANCIS JORDAN JR.,   CORNELIUS STEVENSON
MAXWELL SOMMERVILLE,   JOHN T. MORRIS.

HONORARY VICE-PRESIDENTS.

PROF. F. W. PUTNAM,   . . Massachusetts.
HON. AMOS PERRY, ... Rhode Island.
GEN. J. WATTS DE PEYSTER,   . New York.
HON. R. ALONZO BROCK,   . Virginia.
PROF. JAMES D. BUTLER, ... Wisconsin.

Corresponding Secretary,   BENJ. SMITH LYMAN
Recording Secretary,. .   STEWART CULIN.
Treasurer,   HARRY ROGERS.
Historiographer,   . INMAN HORNER.
Curator of Numismatics, ... F. D. LANGENHEIM.
Curator of Antiquities,   B. N. BAILEY.
Librarian,   CHARLES D. CLARK.

COMMITTEES.

COMMITTEE ON NUMISMATICS.   COMMITTEE ON ANTIQUITIES.

F. D. LANGENHEIM,   CHARLES E. DANA,
J. COLVIN RANDALL,   BENJ. SMITH LYMAN,
HARRY ROGERS.   CORNELIUS STEVENSON.

COMMITTEE ON GENEALOGY.   COMMITTEE ON FINANCE.

WESTCOTT BAILEY,   CHARLES E. DANA,
G. ALBERT LEWIS,   HENRY IUNGERICH,
ELI K. PRICE.   WILLIAM LONGSTRETH

COMMITTEE ON LIBRARY.   COMMITTEE ON HALL.

JOHN M. SCOTT,   FRANKLIN PLATT,
DAVID MILNE,   B. V. MEIN,
CARL EDELHEIM.   FRANCIS JORDAN, JR.

COMMITTEE ON PUBLICATION

STEWART CULIN,   BENJ. SMITH LYMAN,
            MAXWELL SOMMERVILLE.

Hall of the Society, Northwest corner Broad and Pine Sts.

II

1899.

OFFICERS.

PRESIDENT.

DANIEL G. BRINTON, M. D.

VICE-PRESIDENTS.

FRANCIS JORDAN, JR.,   CORNELIUS STEVENSON,
MAXWELL SOMMERVILLE.   JOHN T MORRIS.

HONORARY VICE-PRESIDENTS.

PROF. F. W. PUTNAM, ...   Massachusetts.
HON. AMOS PERRY, ...   Rhode Island
GEN. J. WATTS DE PEYSTER, ...   New York
R. ALONZO BROCK, ESQ., . . .   Virginia.
PROF. JAMES D. BUTLER, . . .   Wisconsin.

Corresponding Secretary.   . BENJ. SMITH LYMAN
Recording Secretary,   . STEWART CULIN.
Treasurer, ... HARRY ROGERS.
Historiographer, ... INMAN HORNER
Curator of Numismatics, ... FREDERICK D. LANGENHEIM.
Curator of Antiquities,   . . . B. N. BAILEY.
Librarian, ... CHARLES D. CLARK.

COMMITTEES.

COMMITTEE ON NUMISMATICS.   COMMITTEE ON ANTIQUITIES.

FREDERICK D. LANGENHEIM,   CHARLES E. DANA,
J. COLVIN RANDALL,   BENJ. SMITH LYMAN.
HARRY ROGERS.   CORNELIUS STEVENSON.

COMMITTEE ON GENEALOGY.   COMMITTEE ON FINANCE.

WESTCOTT BAILEY,   CHARLES E. DANA,
G. ALBERT LEWIS,   HENRY JÜNGERICH,
ELI K. PRICE.   WILLIAM LONGSTRETH.

COMMITTEE ON LIBRARY   COMMITTEE ON HALL.

JOHN M. SCOTT,   FRANKLIN PLATT,
DAVID MILNE,   B. V. MEIN,
CARL EDELHEIM.   FRANCIS JORDAN, JR.

COMMITTEE ON PUBLICATION.

STEWART CULIN,   BENJ. SMITH LYMAN,
MAXWELL SOMMERVILLE.

Hall of the Society, Northwest corner Broad and Pine Sts.

RESIDENT MEMBERS.†

Anderson, Dr. Jos. W., Ardmore, Pa.

Bailey, B. N., 2115 Spruce Street.
Bailey, Westcott, 1020 Chestnut Street.
Baugh, Daniel, Sixteenth and Locust Streets.
Bement, Clarence S., 1804 Spring Garden Street.
Brock, Robert C. H., 1612 Walnut Street.

Clark, Charles D., 2215 Spruce Street.
Clark, Clarence H., S. W cor. Forty-second and Locust Streets.
Cohen, Charles J., 334 South Twenty-first Street.
Colket, C. Howard, 519 Drexel Building.
Cramp, Charles H., 507 South Broad Street.
*Cramp, Henry W., 507 South Broad Street
Culin, Stewart, University of Pennsylvania.

Dana, Charles E., 2013 DeLancey Place.
*Davids, Richard Wistar, 202 Bullitt Building.
Davis, Robert S., 1801 Spruce Street.
Dolan, Thomas, 1809 Walnut Street.

Furness, Frank, 711 Locust Street.

Gans, Leopold, 130 Market Street, Chicago, Ill.
Greenough, E. W., 1804 Pine Street.
Gutekunst, Frederic, 712 Arch Street.

Harrison, Charles C., 400 Chestnut Street.

*Hart, Charles Henry, 1819 Chestnut Street.
Horner, Inman, Rittenhouse Club.
*Hutchinson, Charles H., 1617 Walnut Street.

Iungerich, Henry, 1721 Spruce Street.

Jayne, Dr. Horace, 313 South Nineteenth Street.
Jenks, John Story, 1937 Arch Street.
Jordan, Francis, Jr., 2228 Spruce Street.

Langenheim, F. D., Ardmore, Pa.
Lea, Charles M., 2006 Walnut Street.
Lea, Henry C., 2000 Walnut Street.
Leach, Frank Willing, 254 South Twenty-third Street.
Lewis, G. Albert, 1834 DeLancey Place.
Lewis, Howard W., 427 Chestnut Street.
Lewis, John F., 1908 Spruce Street.
Longstreth, William, 2013 Chestnut Street.
*Lyman, Benj. Smith, 708 South Washington Square.

Mein, B. V., S. E. cor. Dillwyn and Green Streets.
Mercer, Henry C., Doylestown, Pa.
Milne, Caleb J., 2030 Walnut Street.
*Milne, David, 2030 Walnut Street.
*Moore, Clarence B., 1321 Locust Street.
*Morris, John T., 826 Drexel Building.
Myer, Isaac, 21 East Sixtieth Street, New York.

Peirce, George, 623 Walnut Street.
Pfahler, Alfred E., 127 North Thirty-third Street.

14

Pfahler, W. H., 127 North Thirty-
third Street.
Phillips, Wm. B., 1826 Pine Street.
Platt, Franklin, 1820 Chestnut Street.
Price, Eli Kirk, 709 Walnut Street.

Rogers, Harry, 2216 DeLancey Street.

Scott, John M., 116 South Eighteenth
Street.
Sommerville, Maxwell, 311 South
Tenth Street.
Starr, Edward, Wyncote. Pa.
Stevenson, Cornelius, 237 S. Twenty-
first Street.

Todd, M. Hampton, 721 Walnut
Street.
*Toppan, Robert Noxon, 10 Highland
Street, Cambridge, Mass.
Tower, Charlemagne, U. S. Ambassa-
dor, St. Petersburg, Russia.
*Townsend, John W., 2103 Walnut
Street.

*Wagner, H. Dumont,
Wolbert, Charles E., N.E. cor. Twenty-
second and South Streets.
Woodside, Geo. D., 22 South Water
Street.
Wright, Joseph, 2023 Walnut Street.

HONORARY MEMBERS.

Butler, James D., LL. D., Madison, Wis.

Evans, Sir John, K. C. B., Nash Mills, Hemel Hempstead, Eng.

Levasseur, Emil, Paris, France.
Loubat, Le Duc de, Paris, France.

Madden, Frederick W., Brighton, Eng.
Murray, James A. H., London, Eng.
Owen, Sir P. Cunliffe, London, Eng.
Patterson, James W., Hanover, N. H., Director of the U. S. Mint, *ex-officio*.

CORRESPONDING MEMBERS.

Abbott, Charles C., M. D., Bristol, Pa.
Adam, Lucien, Rennes, France.
Adams, Dr. Herbert B., Baltimore, Md.
Ambiveri, Prof. Luigi, Milan, Italy.
Appleton, William S., Boston, Mass.
Axon, W. A. E., Manchester, Eng.
Aymé, Louis H., Merida, Yucatan.

Bancroft, Hubert Howe, San Francisco, Cal.
Barber, Edwin A., West Chester, Pa.
Beauchamp, W. M., Baldwinsville, N. Y.
Bergsöe, Vilhelm, Copenhagen, Denmark.
Boas, Franz, Cambridge, Mass.
Bolton, H. Carrington, Washington, D. C.
Broadhead, Luke W., Delaware Water Gap, Pa.
Brock, Robert Alonzo, Richmond, Va.
Brooks, Rev. William Henry, Hanover, Mass.
Brown, John Marshall, Portland, Me.
Brühl, Gustav, Cincinnati, O.
Bryant, Hubbard Winslow, Portland, Me.
Bulliott, J. G., Autun, France.

Cannizzaro, Tommaso, Messina, Italy.
Carutti di Cantogno, Baron Domenico, Turin, Italy.
Clarke, Robert, Cincinnati, O.
Comfort, Aaron J., M. D., Milwaukee, Wis.
Cope, Gilbert, West Chester, Pa.
Cournault, Chas., Malzéville, France.
Cushing, Frank Hamilton, Washington, D. C.

Darling, Gen. C. W., Utica, N. Y.
Da Silva, Chev. I., Lisbon, Portugal.
Davenport, Henry, Boston, Mass.
Davis, W. W. H., Doylestown, Pa.
Dean, John Ward, Boston, Mass.
Deans, James, Victoria, B. C.
De Charency, Comte Hyacinthe, St. Maurice Les Charency, France.
De Clève, Jules, Mons, Belgium.
De Costa, Rev. B. F., New York, N. Y.
Del Mar, Alexander, San Francisco, Cal.
De Madrazo, Pedro, Madrid, Spain.
De Olaguibel, Manuel, Mexico.
De Peyster, Gen. J. Watts, Tivoli, Duchess Co., N. Y.

15

De Rochambeau, Marquis A., Paris, France.
De Rosny, Léon, Paris, France.
Devilliers, Léopold, Mons, Belgium.
Di Cesnola, Gen. Louis P., New York, N. Y.
Donner, Dr.Otto, Helsingfors,Finland.
Durand, John, Paris, France.

Egle, William H., M. D., Harrisburg, Pa.

Field, Osgood, Rome, Italy.
Forchheimer, Eduard,Vienna,Austria.

Gatschet, Albert S., Washington, D. C.
Giglioli, Henry H., Florence, Italy.
Gilman, Daniel C., Baltimore, Md.
Glatz, A. Hiestand, York. Pa.
Goodyear, Prof. William H., Brooklyn, N. Y.
Green, Samuel A., M. D., Boston, Mass.
Griffin, Rev. Geo. H., Springfield, Mass.

Hadi, Syad Mohammed, Sultanpur, India.
Hamy, Dr. E. T., Paris, France.
Harden, William, Savannah, Ga.
Hayden, Rev. Horace Edwin, Wilkesbarre, Pa.
Haynes, Henry W., Boston, Mass.
Head, Barclay V., London, Eng.
Herbst, C. F., Copenhagen, Denmark.
Herndon, William H.,Springfield, Ill.
Hickox, John H., Washington, D. C.
Hildebrand, Hans Olof H.. Stockholm, Sweden.
Holmes, Nathaniel, Cambridge, Mass.
Horner, Frederick, Jr.. M. D., Marshall, Fauquier Co., Va.
Howard, Jos. Jackson, London, Eng.
Huguet-Latour, Major L. A., Montreal, Canada.

Imhoof-Blumer, F.,Winterthur, Switzerland.
Im Thurn, E. F., Georgetown, British Guiana.

Jenkins, Howard M., Gwynedd, Pa.

Karabacek, Prof. Josef, Vienna, Aus.
Keary, C. F., London, England.
Kenner, Dr. Frederick, Vienna, Aus.
Koehler, S. R., Boston, Mass.
Konstostaulas, A., Athens, Greece.

Krause, Prof. W., Berlin, Germany.
Krauss, Dr. Friedrich S., Vienna, Aus.

Leibert, Rev. Eugene, Nazareth, Pa.
Le Moine, J. M., Quebec, Canada.
Lincoln, Frederick William, London, Eng.
Lindsley, John Berrien, M. D., Nashville, Tenn.
Long, Rev. Albert L., Constantinople, Turkey.
Loring, Gen. Chas. G., Boston, Mass.
Low, Lyman H., New York, N. Y.
Lubbock, Sir John, London, Eng.

Machado y Alvarez, Dr. Antonio, Madrid, Spain.
March, Prof. Francis A., Easton, Pa.
Marvin, W. T. R., Boston, Mass.
Mason, Otis T., Washington, D. C.
Meltzl de Lomnitz. Dr. Hugo, Klausenburg, Austria.
Mercur, Rodney A., Towanda, Pa.
Merzbacher, Dr. Eugen, Munich, Germany.
Meyer, C., Hamburg, Germany.
Mitchell,Arthur, Edinburgh,Scotland.
Morse, Prof. Edward S., Salem, Mass.
Mott, Henry, Montreal, Canada.
Much, Dr. M., Vienna, Austria.

Nadaillac, Le Marquis de, Paris, France.
Nicolaysen, N., Christiania, Norway.
Norton, Charles Eliot, Cambridge, Mass.
Nuttall, Mrs. Zelia, Dresden,Germany.

Paine. Nathaniel, Worcester, Mass.
Peñafiel, Antonio, Mexico.
Poillon, William. Chicago, Ill.
Pomjalowski. Prof. Ivan V., St. Petersburg, Russia.
Ponce de Leon, Nestor, New York, N. Y.
Post, George E., M. D., Smyrna, Turkey.
Putnam, Prof. Fred. W., Cambridge, Mass.

Read, Chas. H., London, Eng.
Riggauer, Dr. Hans, Munich, Germany.
Robinson, Geo. E., Cardiff, Wales.
Rogers, Rev. Charles, London, Eng.

Salisbury, Stephen, Worcester, Mass.
Sanchez, Jesus, Mexico.
Sandham, Alfred, Montreal, Canada.
Seletti, Emilio, Milan, Italy.
Sergi, Prof. Giuseppe, Rome, Italy
Serrure, Raymond, Paris, France.
Seymour, Frederick H., Detroit,
Mich.
Sharpless, Alfred, West Chester, Pa.
Sharpless, Philip P., West Chester,
Pa.
Six van Hillegom, Dr. J. P., Amster-
dam, Holland.
Slafter, Rev. Edmund F., Boston,
Mass.
Stevens, John Austin, New York,
N. Y.
Stiles, Henry R., M. D., Hillview,
Warren Co., N. Y.
Strong, Herbert A., LL. D., Melbourne,
Australia.
Sweeny, Robert O., M. D., Duluth,
Minn.
Szombathy, Josef, Vienna, Austria.

Thomas, Thomas H., Cardiff, Wales.
Thorsteinson, Arni, Reykjavik, Ice-
land.
Thruston, Gates P., Nashville, Tenn.
Tooker, Wm. Wallace, Sag Harbor,
L. I., N. Y.
Trask, Wm. Blake, Boston, Mass.
Trau, Franz, Vienna, Austria.
Tylor, Dr. Edward B., Oxford, Eng.

Von Ernst, Carl, Vienna, Austria.
Von Raimann, Dr. Franz, Vienna,
Austria.
Von Tiesenhausen, Prof. Vladimir, St.
Petersburg, Russia.
Vors, Frederick, New York, N. Y.

Wauvermans, Lt.-Gen. Henry, Brus-
sels, Belgium.
Williams, J. Fletcher, St. Paul, Minn.
Wilmersdörffer, Max, Munich, Ger-
many.
Winks, Rev. William E., Cardiff,
Wales.

DONORS TO THE LIBRARY 1892-98.

(I) INDIVIDUALS.

Ambiveri, Prof. L., Milan, Italy.
Atkinson, Edward, Boston, Mass.

Bolton, H. C., New York, N. Y.
Borton, E. M. Worcester, Mass.
Bourke, Capt. John G., U. S. A., Ft.
    Ethan Allen, Vt.
Bowker, R. R., New York, N. Y.
Bradlee, Rev. Dr. Caleb D., Boston,
    Mass.
Brinton, Dr. Daniel G., Media, Pa.
Brock, R. Alonzo, Richmond, Va.
Brock, R. C. H., Philadelphia, Pa.
Butler, Dr. Jas. D., Madison, Wis.
Childs, George W., Philadelphia, Pa.
Culin, Stewart, Philadelphia, Pa.

Darling, Gen. C. W., Utica, N. Y.
Dean, John Ward, Boston, Mass.
De Beaujeu, Monongahéla, Montreal,
    Canada.
De Peyster, Gen. J. Watts, Tivoli, N. Y.
Doggett, Samuel B., Boston, Mass.
Dorsey, J. Owen, Takoma Park, D. C.
Doughty, Francis Worcester, Brook-
    lyn, N. Y.

Field, Osgood, Rome, Italy.
French, A. D. Weld, Boston, Mass.

Gallinger, J. H., U. S. Senate, Wash-
    ington, D. C.
Gatschet, A. S., Washington, D. C.
Gookin, F. W., Chicago, Ill.
Green, Dr. Samuel A., Boston, Mass.

Hamy, Dr. E. T., Paris, France.
Harrison, Dr. W P., Nashville, Tenn.
Hayden, Rev. Horace E., Wilkesbarre,
    Pa.

Henkel, Stanislas V., Philadelphia,
    Pa.

Jackson, Dr. Henry R., Savannah,
    Ga.
Johnson, T. L., M. C., Washington,
    D. C.
Jones, Chas. C., Augusta, Ga.
Jones, Chas. E., Augusta, Ga.
Jones, Dr. Jos., New Orleans, La.

Kervey, H. Rush, West Chester, Pa.
Koehler, S. R., Boston, Mass.

Le Moine, J. McPherson, Quebec,
    Canada.
Levasseur, Emil, Paris, France.
Lewis, Hon. Virgil A., Charleston, W.
    Va.
Lindsley, Dr. J. Berrien, Nashville,
    Tenn.
Low, Hon. Seth, New York, N. Y.

Mallery, Col. Garrick, Washington,
    D. C.
Meili, Julius, Zurich, Switzerland.
Mercer, Henry C., Doylestown, Pa.
Moore, Clarence B., Philadelphia,
    Pa.
Morse, Prof. E. S., Salem, Mass.
Myer, Isaac, New York, N Y.

Paine, Nathaniel, Worcester, Mass.
Phillips, G. M., West Chester, Pa.
Piette, Ed., Rumigny, Ardennes,
    France.
Pope, Col. A. A., Boston, Mass.
Putnam, Eben, Salem, Mass.
Putnam, Prof. F W., Cambridge,
    Mass.

18

Roest, Th. M., Leyden, Holland.

Schlegel, Gustav, Leyden, Holland.
Seletti, E., Milan, Italy
Seltman, E. J., London, Eng.
Seymour, F. H., Detroit, Mich.
Shafter, Rev. Edmund F., Boston, Mass.
Storer, Dr. H. R., Newport, R. I.

Tatman, Chas. T., Worcester, Mass.
Tooker, Wm. Wallace, Sag Harbor,
    N. Y.

Toppan, Robt. Noxon, Cambridge,
    Mass.

Von Hoefken, Rudolf, Vienna, Austria.
Von Tiesenhausen, Prof. Vladimir, St
    Petersburg, Russia.
Voorhees, D. W., U. S. Senate, Wash-
    ington, D. C

Williams, J. Fletcher, St. Paul, Minn.
Winsor, Justin, Cambridge, Mass.
Wood, Isaac F., Rahway, N. J.

(II) SOCIETIES AND INSTITUTIONS.

IN FOREIGN COUNTRIES.

China Branch of the Royal Asiatic Society, Shanghae, China.
Bataviaasch Genootschap v. Kunst u. Wetensch., Batavia, Java.
L'Institut Egyptien, Cairo, Egypt.
Société Impériale Archéologique, St. Petersburg, Russia.
Société Finno-Ougrienne, Helsingfors, Finland.
Kongl. Vitterhets Historie och Antiq. Akad., Stockholm, Sweden.
Numismatische Gesellschaft, Berlin, Germany.
Deutsche Zeitschrift für Geschichtswissenschaft, Freiburg, Baden.
Alterthums-Verein, Munich, Germany.
Numismatische Gesellschaft, Vienna, Austria.
Hrvatsko Starinarsko Druztvo, Knin, Dalmatia, Austria.
Moniteur International, Liége, Belgium.
La Gazette Numismatique, Brussels, Belgium.
Cercle Archéologique de Mons, Belgium.
Musée Guimet, Paris, France.
Société d'Anthropologie, Paris, France.
Société des Américanistes, Paris, France.
Société d'Ethnographie, Paris, France.
Société Philologique, Paris, France.
Société d'Emulation des Côtes-du-Nord, St. Brieuc, France.
R. Accademia di Scienze, Lettere e Belle Arti, Palermo, Italy.
Academia Real das Sciencias, Lisbon, Portugal.
Philosophical Society of Glasgow, Scotland.
Cambridge Antiquarian Society, Cambridge, Eng.
Athenæum, London, Eng.

City of London Library Committee, London, Eng.
R. Society of Antiquaries of Ireland, Dublin, Ireland.
Société de Numismatique et d'Archéologie de Montréal, Canada.
Historical and Scientific Society of Manitoba, Winnipeg, Man.
Direccion General de la Estadística de la Republica Mexicana, Mexico, Mexico.

IN THE UNITED STATES.

Bangor Historical Society, Bangor, Me.
Library Association, Portland, Me.
Essex Institute, Salem, Mass.
Commonwealth Publishing Co., Boston, Mass.
Museum of Fine Arts, Boston, Mass.
Public Library, Boston, Mass.
Old South Studies in History, Boston, Mass.
Peabody Museum, Cambridge, Mass.
American Humane Association, Providence, R. I.
Rhode Island Historical Society, Providence, R. I.
New Haven Historical Society, New Haven, Conn.
American Metrological Society, New York, N. Y.
American Museum of Natural History, New York, N. Y.
American Numismatic and Archaeological Society, New York, N. Y.
Fleming H Revell Co., New York, N. Y.
Independent, New York, N. Y.
International News Co., New York, N. Y.
N. Y. Society, Founders and Patriots of America, New York, N. Y.
Political Science Publishing Co., New York, N. Y.
Yonkers Histor. and Library Asso., Yonkers, N. Y.

Lake Mohonk Conference, Mohonk Lake, N. Y.

Oneida Historical Society, Utica, N. Y.

Buffalo Historical Society, Buffalo, N. Y.

New Jersey Historical Society, Newark, N. J

American Historical Register, Philadelphia, Pa.

American Philosophical Society, Philadelphia, Pa.

American Society for Extension of Univ Teaching, Philadelphia, Pa.

Fairmount Park Art Association, Philadelphia, Pa.

Literary Era, Philadelphia, Pa.

Penna. Museum and School of Industrial Art, Philadelphia, Pa.

University of Penna. Botanical Laboratory, Philadelphia, Pa.

University of Penna. Dept. of Archæology and Palæont., Philadelphia, Pa.

University of Penna. Dept. of History, Philadelphia, Pa.

Lackawanna Institute of History and Science, Scranton, Pa.

Wyoming Commemorative Association, Wilkesbarre, Pa.

Wyoming Historical and Geological Society, Wilkesbarre, Pa.

Lancaster Daily Intelligencer, Lancaster, Pa.

Historical Society of Dauphin County, Harrisburg, Pa.

American Historical Association, Washington, D. C.

Anthropological Society of Washington, D. C.

Smithsonian Institution, Washington, D. C.

United States Bureau of Education, Washington, D. C.

United States Bureau of Ethnology, Washington, D. C.

United States Census Office, Washington, D. C.

United States Civil Service Commission, Washington, D. C.

United States Department of State, Washington, D C.

United States National Museum, Washington, D. C.

Alabama Historical Society, Carrollton, Ala.

Western Reserve Historical Society, Cleveland, O.

American Archæologist, Columbus, O.

Ohio Archæological and Historical Society, Columbus, O.

Woman's Home Companion, Springfield, O.

Field Columbian Museum, Chicago, Ill.

Library Bureau, Chicago, Ill.

Literary Club, Chicago, Ill.

Pullman Palace Car Co., Chicago, Ill.

Wisconsin Academy of Arts and Science, Madison, Wis.

Wisconsin State Historical Society, Madison, Wis.

Iowa Masonic Library, Cedar Rapids, Ia.

Academy of Science, St. Louis, Mo.

Nebraska State Historical Society, Lincoln, Neb.

Kansas Academy of Science, Topeka, Kan.

Kansas State Historical Society, Topeka, Kan.

Kansas University, Lawrence, Kan.

Colorado College Scientific Society, Colorado Springs, Col.

Historical Society of the State of Montana, Helena, Mon.

Pacific Northwest, Portland, Ore.

Library Association, Portland, Ore.

University of California, Berkeley, Cal.

Los Angeles Saturday Times, Los Angeles, Cal.

DONORS TO THE CABINET 1892-98.

Allen, Mrs. Harrison, Philadelphia.

Brinton, Dr. Daniel G., Media, Pa.

Brock, R. A., Richmond, Va.

Columbia University, New York City.

Culin, Stewart, Philadelphia.

Darling, Gen. C. W., Utica, N. Y.

Eyre, Charles, Florence, Italy.

Farnum, J. Edward, Philadelphia.

Green, Dr. Samuel A., Boston, Mass.

Horner, Inman, Philadelphia.

Iüngerich, H., Philadelphia.

Lamborn, Dr. Robert H., Philadelphia.

Langenheim, F. D., Ardmore, Pa.

Macauley, Francis C., Florence, Italy.

Moore, Clarence B., Philadelphia.

Poillon, William, Chicago, Ill.

Randall, J. Colvin, Philadelphia.

Roest, M. T., Leyden, Holland.

Spanish Government, The.

Sutton, L. J.

Takayanagi, Tozo, New York City.

Wyoming Historical and Geological Society, Wilkesbarre, Pa.

PROCEEDINGS.

JANUARY 7TH.

Mr. Culin read a paper entitled, "The Popular Literature of the Chinese in the United States," * illustrated by a collection of books purchased in the Chinese shops in Philadelphia and New York City. Mr. Culin exhibited a collection of Chinese coins and medals, the property of the Board of Foreign Missions of the Presbyterian Church, including a large number of irregularly shaped pieces; one, probably intended as an amulet, in the form of a small bell. The collection also comprised the usual types of "razor," "key," and "cloth" coins, and a set of eight medals, with representations and the names of the Eight Genii. Doubt was expressed as to the antiquity of many of the specimens; for the uniformity of the patina appeared to be the result of some artificial process rather than of age.

Mr. Harry Rogers exhibited a Japanese ivory carving in the form of a pipe case with a pendant box. It was composed of many pieces hinged upon a framework.

The committee on the collection of objects for the Madrid Exhibition in 1892 was continued. The Society also agreed to loan its collection of Peruvian idols to the Loan Exhibition of Religious Objects at the University Museum. Included in this collection is a mold for making clay idols from Chancay.

A letter from the Rev. Albert L. Long, of Robert College, Constantinople, a Corresponding Member of the Society, was read, in which he referred to a tablet from the Grand Bazaar, Constantinople, with an inscription in Greek characters, which was illustrated in the last report of the Society's Proceedings (for 1887-89) for the purpose of obtaining information about it. No one had been able to translate the inscription. Mr. Long said:

---

* Published in *Oriental Studies*, by the Oriental Club of Philadelphia. Boston, 1894.

23

"I recognize an old acquaintance in the lithographed inscription on page 67 of the report. It has been known to me for some time. I knew very well the man who, I believe, made it. He is dead, poor fellow! but a good many specimens of his work still remain in the markets. I have seen some of them even in European museums. I had missed this stone from its accustomed place and had wondered what had become of it."

FEBRUARY 4TH, 1892.

Capt. R. S. Collum, Assistant Quartermaster, U. S. M. C., read a paper on "The Aborigines of North America, and Their Relation to the Aborigines of Japan."

(ABSTRACT.)

In favor of the Japanese origin of the American Indians there are arguments from the drift of ocean currents, island stepping-stones, physiognomy, and ethnic traits.

The ocean currents must have frequently carried boats and men northward from the Malay Archipelago along the shores of Japan; where the Ainos had spread southward from Sagalin and the continent, later to be driven back northward by conquerors from the mainland of Southern Asia, yet leaving behind Aino names of places and prehistoric relics of the Stone Age. Further northward, the Japanese ocean current—the *Kuro Shio*, or Black Brine—is known to have carried forty-nine junks to the neighborhood of the American, or even beyond to the Hawaiian shores, in the ninety-four years from 1782 to 1876. Dr. Brinton, in his excellent work, *The American Race*, has admitted that "it is not impossible that in recent centuries some junks may have drifted on the northwest coast;" though he does not think the fact offers any solution of the problem. The similarity of the fauna and flora of the two coasts is due, not to a former land connection, but to the Japan current.

Again, from Yesso to Kamchatka the Kurile Islands stretch like the ruins of a causeway, prolonged by the Aleutian Islands to Alaska. Among the wandering tribes of Siberia there are traditions of the departure of ancestors northeastward across the sea filled with ice.

Arguments from physiognomy are not wanting. Griffis found

photographs of Colorado and Nebraska Indians to be mistaken by Japanese for pictures of their own countrymen. Retzius and Humboldt find "the Pacific Coast Indians related to the Mongols, and their skulls bear strong resemblance to the Mongol Kalmucks." Catlin found among the western Indians strongly marked traces of Mongolian origin. W. H. Seward declares the tribes of Alaska to be "manifestly of Mongol origin."

Similarities in the languages, customs, superstitions, and religions also bear witness to the single origin of the races of the two continents. In the Indian vocabularies unaltered Japanese words have been found. The sacred mask-dances and the worship of the sun and of the forces of nature are instances of a strong likeness between Japan and America. In the Aztec and Japanese zodiac, six of the elements agree in both. Phallic worship has been observed in Japan similar to that of the American Indians. The characteristic Japanese fox-myths have their parallel in those of the coyote on the American Pacific coast. Furthermore, the Indian totems and the Japanese badges have a striking resemblance. The manner of life in Alaska is similar to that of the aborigines of Japan; and the myths of the Alaska Indians resemble those of Japan. Dr. Sheldon Jackson pronounces the Alaskan tribes, in mental traits, artistic ideas, and methods of labor, singularly like the Mongolian Japanese. Dr. Robertson, in the last century, says the American Indians came from Tartary in Asia.

In the discussion following the reading of the paper, Dr. D. G. Brinton admitted the evidence presented by Captain Collum, but called attention to the fact of great differences of a linguistic character. He held that the chain of the Aleutian Islands could not have been stepping-stones to the American continent, because the most western of them were found unpopulated by early navigators, who also found evidences of the arts and customs of the American Indians on the eastern islands. Bering Strait, he admitted, could have been a highway of communication.

All actual evidence from tradition, language and arts confirms the opinion that the migration of tribes has been from time immemorial *from* America *into* Asia, and not in the reverse direction. The earliest navigators found Eskimo families dwelling on the shores of Asia; but no Siberian tribes in Alaska. The ascertained direction of Eskimo wanderings has always been from south to north and from east to west. Slaves and other objects of barter were conveyed across the straits to the American shore, which explains the presence of Asian manufactured objects and of an Asian physiognomy in some tribes of the northwest coast; but no trace of the Japanese or Aino or of any Ural-Altaic tongue has been reported in America on sufficient testimony to make the assertion worth combating.

Dr. Charles C. Abbott said that his careful study of the Delaware Valley led him to the conclusion that there had been a distinct progress among the aborigines of the Atlantic coast, beginning at a very low stage. At such a low stage it would seem impossible for people to have traveled across the continent, so that for the original peopling of the Atlantic coast we must look to Europe.

March 3d, 1892.

President Daniel G. Brinton read a paper entitled, "Mediæval and Aboriginal Dramas," in which he contrasted the miracle plays of Europe with the plays of the American Indians.

Mr. Culin read a paper on "Old Chinese Graves in Philadelphia."

Mr. Culin exhibited several amulets from the collection of the Museum of Archæology of the University of Pennsylvania, recently presented by Mrs. John Harrison and collected by her in the East in 1889 and 1890. One, a green stone talisman, purchased at Jaffa, bore an inscription in Arabic of Cufic type, reading "God is High." Another was a small metal hand stamped with a Hebrew inscription, worn on the forehead by Jewish boys in Cairo to keep off the evil eye. The inscription, as translated by Dr. Morris Jastrow, reads *Ben Pôrath Jôsêf*: "a young branch is Joseph" (Gen. xlix, 22). *Shaddai*, and "Jerusalem, the Holy City." This gave rise to a discussion in which the widespread use of the extended hand as a magical symbol was referred to. It extends across the entire continent of Asia, reaching to Japan, and reappears in America. Mr. Charles E. Dana spoke of the custom in Cairo, when a funeral passes, of putting out two fingers of one hand and crying, "You go first, and I'll follow after." Mr. Herbert Friedenwald stated that it was common to see the horses and donkeys in Cairo stamped with a red hand with henna. He stated also that the position of the hands in the dance of the Dervishes was an important characteristic.

Mr. Inman Horner exhibited an interesting collection of coins, loaned for the occasion by Dr. S. Emlen Meigs, comprising a twenty-shilling piece of Charles II, containing 1858 grains of silver, 925 fine; a siege piece of the city of Leyden, with the arms of the city and the motto, *Pugno Pro Patria*, and a siege piece of the same city struck in papier maché. Also, several restruck pieces, one of the Russian Mint.

Mr. Harry Rogers presented to the Society a set of the new silver and base coinage recently made by the Chinese Government at Canton.

April 7th, 1892.

The death of Thomas Hockley, Treasurer of the Society since 1888, was announced, March 12th, 1892, in his 54th year.

Mr. Inman Horner read the following paper on "The Intercontinental Trade of Bering Straits:"

THE INTER-CONTINENTAL TRADE OF BERING STRAITS.

By Inman Horner.

The immediate cause for reading this paper is my conversations with Lieutenant Miles C. Gorgas, U. S. N., who spent three years in Alaskan waters on the U. S. Steamer "Bear," and who was an eye-witness of the fairs and marts by which the commerce is carried on.

Nordenskjöld, in his famous trip along the north coast of Asia, gives ample testimony of how far-reaching this traffic was among the Chuckhis of Eastern Asia. He left Karlskrona on the 22d of June, 1878, in the "Vega," and passing into the Arctic seas, endeavored to coast along the Asiatic continent to Bering Straits. He was almost successful in the effort in one summer season, but, fortunately perhaps for science, he was compelled to pass a dreary winter within a few miles short of the Straits. The "Vega" was frozen in the ice near Koliuchin Bay, in 67° 4' north latitude and 173° 23' west from Greenwich, on September 29th, 1878; the distance from East Cape, the easternmost point of Asia, being 120 miles, and from Point Hope, the opposite American land, 180 miles.

The Swedish navigators made many sledge journeys and a careful examination of the natives. The Chuckchis had been first met on September 6th, near Bear Island, many miles further west. It was remarked that none of them could speak Russian, but that a boy could count in English up to ten, which Nordenskjöld puts down to the influence of American whalers. On September 7th Nordenskjöld encountered two large boat-loads of men, women, and children and began to barter with them. I quote him verbatim, page 332: "The Chuckchis wherever met were found using American tobacco and spirits, which last they called *ram* from the English word 'rum.' They have sail-cloth and guns made in America. During the winter, but especially in the spring, sledges drawn by dogs, traveling eastward to Bering Straits, were constantly stopping for a friendly visit to the 'Vega.' They were heavily laden with furs, principally reindeer skins, and were bound, the owners said, for the markets near Bering Straits." What I have cited, as well as the fact that the Chuckchis had no idea of money, refusing to accept silver coins unless they were bored for medals, shows how large a part barter played in the lives of this Asiatic polar race.

The "Vega" remained imbedded in the ice until June 18th, 1879, when with flags flying she steamed into the Straits dividing the old world and the new. On the 21st of July he visited Port Clarence, on the American side, and gives a lively and picturesque account of the harbor and scene there:

"The Chuckchis are otherwise shrewd and calculating men of business. They have been brought up to this from childhood through the barter they carry on between America and Siberia. Many a beaver-skin that comes to the market at Irbit (Siberia) belongs to an animal that has been caught in America, whose skin has been passed from hand to hand among the wild men of America until it finally reaches the Russian market. For this barter a sort of market is held on an island in Bering Straits. At the most remote markets in Polar America a beaver skin is said, some years ago, to have been occasionally exchanged for a leaf of tobacco."

On page 487, he says: "According to von Dittmar, there exists, or still existed in 1856, a steady, slow but regular transport of goods along the whole north coast of Asia and America by which Russian goods were conveyed to the innermost parts of Polar America, and furs found their way to the bazaars of Moscow and St. Petersburg."

The inhabitants were almost altogether Eskimo, but there were a few Chuckchis. The natives lived in cotton cloth tents during the summer and had European clothes. They even had mats from the Sandwich Islands and all sorts of American guns and hardware. He saw a piece of nephrite which he thought must have been brought in a prehistoric stone age from Central Asia, pointing to the immense antiquity of the circumpolar trade.

The destination of the reindeer skins can be traced on the map of westernmost Alaska. They are carried across Bering Straits, a distance of less than fifty miles, to Port Clarence, where are assembled in June the inhabitants of that part of America; the American whaling ships, on their way to the fishing ground, having by that time landed tobacco, spirits, sail-cloth, cutlery, etc. This is the earliest of the great annual gatherings of the traders of the Peninsula.

There appear to be four annual fairs held in the extreme north-

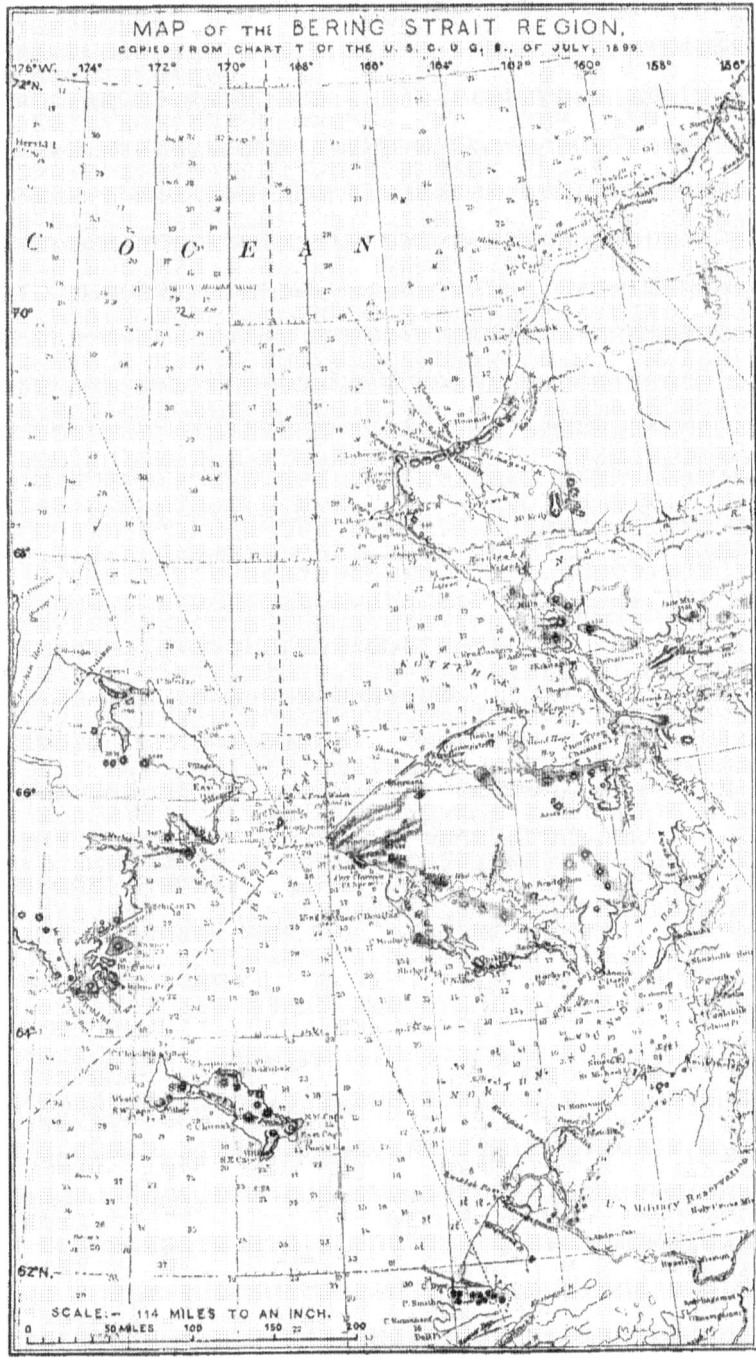

MAP OF THE BERING STRAIT REGION.
COPIED FROM CHART T OF THE U. S. C. U. G. S., OF JULY, 1899.

SCALE:— 114 MILES TO AN INCH.

western part of Alaska, that is, at or near Bering Straits, or on the north shore, between the straits and the mouth of the Mackenzie River. Beginning at the southernmost, a fair is held in June at Port Clarence, just south of the narrowest part of the Straits. It is attended by the inhabitants of St. Lawrence Island, south of the Straits; by Siberians of the Chuckchi tribe, and by Indians from Cape Prince of Wales, the westernmost land of North America. They make their way from these different islands and capes of the two continents in their large, open boats, called *oomiaks*, and come in families, men, women and children. Their boats are drawn up on the beach and their camp is made under the lee of the boat turned on its side, with a skin, or, at present, cotton duck, for additional shelter.

The object of the fair is to procure from the whalers flour, tobacco, cotton duck for tents, powder and whisky. The Siberians bring the skins of reindeer, and the Americans furs, for barter. They wait for the whalers, who appear as soon as the ice breaks, on their way up to the cruising grounds. They live on blubber. Each man trades for himself, and each tribe keeps its own quarters in the camp, apart from the others.

Proceeding northward through Bering Strait, we find at Hotham Inlet, on Kotzebue Sound, the largest fair. The annual attendance here is computed at 1,500 men, women, and children. It lasts through July and August. The people live under the shelter of tents, as well as under that of their boats. The Siberians are not very numerous here, but there are large bodies of Indians from the interior. Those who have spent June at the Port Clarence Fair arrive at Kotzebue to trade off the Siberian products obtained by barter. They also bring with them flour and cotton duck obtained from the whalers, who seldom do any trading inside the Straits. The Point Hope Indians, on the north shore, attend this fair in large numbers. The principal traders of the whole region are the Prince of Wales Indians, who carry the skins of the Siberians and the supplies to the Kotzebue Sound fair. The skins of tame reindeer, which are much prized as clothing, are passed thus from Bering Straits. Other articles in use all along the north coast which are distributed by these intertribal fairs, are waterproof boots, for hard work, made of seal skin by the St. Lawrence Indians, and dry boots, so called, made with many ornaments, which are highly valued by Indian dandies.

There are also fairs at Point Lay, or Kokolik, between Point

Hope and Point Barrow, and at Camden Bay, 450 miles east of Point Barrow, and half way to the mouth of the Mackenzie. The one at Point Lay is attended by the Point Hope men.

The appearance of the fair at Hotham Inlet may be described as follows: It is a land-locked bay, with a shingle and sand beach. On the beach, just where the short grass shows itself, there is a confused array of tents made of cotton duck, others of reindeer skin, and others of scantling and driftwood, and of *oomiaks* lying on their sides, with a flap of duck or skin. On the beach, near the water, are the *kayaks*. Near each tent are the Eskimo dogs, six or seven of which have been used in tracking the boats in summer and the sleds in winter. The people are dressed in all kinds of garments, from reindeer furs to red flannel underclothes. Their receptacle for furs is the whole skin of a hair seal, with a slit in the stomach, serving as a trunk. The Indians are coming and going all the time. This is the great business mart of all the northwest coast, where the Indians exchange their own products for the necessaries or luxuries made by their neighbors, either of Asia or America, or brought by whalers. All exchanges are made by barter, as they have nothing like money, or even a standard, as skins or cattle, wampum or cowries.

This commerce has in all probability been carried on for generations. We can hardly estimate for how long. The whalers have to some extent changed the character of the goods dealt in, but did not originate the meeting of the traders at these northern harbors. Long before sails appeared in Bering Sea, Asiatics and Americans were meeting to barter peacefully the products of one continent for the products of the other.

President Brinton, in commenting upon this paper, said that it was an important contribution to science, and that while the existence of one fair had been known, the information as to the others was entirely new. Mr. Horner exhibited a collection of Eskimo objects, collected by Lieutenant Gorgas.*

A highly important collection of Alaskan objects,† collected by Mr. Joseph G. Rosengarten, was also exhibited. Many of

---

* This collection has since been deposited in the Archæological Museum of the University of Pennsylvania.

† Now in the Museum of Archæology of the University of Pennsylvania.

them were of a symbolic or religious character, including a ceremonial arrow, wrapped with porcupine quills, with a stone point, a drum used in dances, and three charms suspended by cords, one of which was a crescent-shaped stone, bearing upon one side a fish inscribed in red, and on the other a Greek cross surrounded with seven dots, overarched with two curved lines. These devices were regarded as representing the four directions, the stars of the Great Bear and the firmament. Another object, representing a raven holding a mask before its breast, was of peculiar interest, as, according to President Brinton, it represented the great bird, a raven or crow, to which, in the myths of most of the northwest coast tribes, was attributed the creation of the world. "The dark storm clouds are spoken of as the shadows of its wings and the thunder as the noise of their flapping. This demiurgic bird is still the mystic source of life. The present specimen shows it holding in its hands a mask; in other words, the head of a person who is masked for the sacred ceremony, and it is vitalizing him, as in the act of brooding. It is remarkable that precisely the same symbolism is the explanation of the 'winged globe,' so frequent on Egyptian monuments."

Mr. Harry Rogers was elected Treasurer, to fill the unexpired term of the deceased Treasurer.

MAY 5TH, 1892.

Mr. Inman Horner exhibited an additional series of objects collected in Alaska by Lieutenant Miles C. Gorgas, U. S. N. It comprised two bows reinforced with sinew, bone-tipped arrows, a harpoon with detachable bone point, and a set of Indian gambling sticks.

Mr. Culin read a paper on "The Romantic Literature of the Chinese in the United States."

JULY 7TH, 1892.

Mr. Culin was appointed delegate of the Society to the Historico-American Exposition at Madrid and the Congress of Americanists at Huelva, Spain. He was authorized to take with him to the Madrid Exhibition a collection of the Society's medals and paper money.

3

Mr. Lyman was requested to act as Recording Secretary during Mr. Culin's absence at the Madrid Exhibition.

The death of Sir Daniel Wilson, Corresponding Member, August 7th, was announced.

The President, Dr. D. G. Brinton, spoke of the group of fifty or sixty so-called Indian pits, aboriginal quarries of black chert and jasper, in the Durham and Reading Hills, near Vera Cruz, ten or fifteen miles southwesterly from Allentown; and of a like group, twice as numerous, a mile and a half from Macungie, on the East Pennsylvania Railroad, in Lehigh County, and eight miles southwesterly from Allentown.

The pits near Vera Cruz surpass in extent those of Flint Ridge, Licking County, Ohio, and are thirty or forty feet in diameter and from five to fifteen feet deep, and a number are one hundred feet long by twenty feet wide and about fifteen feet deep. They were dug by the aborigines for black chert and jasper to be made into arrow-heads; and follow well-marked jasper veins, supposed to be in or near the Laurentian gneiss, and running about north and south, at right angles with the general trend of the hills. The jasper is in nodules about two feet in diameter; and was broken at first by fire or by blows. Some specimens are rosy jasper and some yellowish. The material was thrown as refuse to the side of the pit, or was carried to a distant point and worked. The fact that there are no mounds around the pit to compare with the extent of the excavations shows that large quantities of material were carried away. One work-shop site was found at a quarter or half a mile from the pits; and many chips and "rejects" were found there, and one small broken but well formed pebble hammer about an inch and a half in diameter, of diorite, or like stone, not of the quarry material. Not a single arrow-head, however, was found, except one of quartzite brought from elsewhere. A mile from the work-shop was found a village site with hearths and flint chips.

Five specimens of "rejects" from two of the quarries were exhibited; and all show that they were vitiated by a roundish hump or bulge on one side, making it impossible to complete a good arrow-head from them. They closely resemble all the so-called paleolithic implements of America, and even those of Europe. It is argued by Mr W. H Holmes that all American so-called paleoliths are simply such rejects of a skilled manufacture, and that they do not necessarily indicate a stage of culture inferior to that of the most advanced stone age. It is hoped that further examination of these quarries will throw more light on this interesting question.

The President had visited the Vera Cruz pits this day in company with Mr. H. C. Mercer, of Doylestown, and Mr. Charlemagne Tower, Jr., President of the Board of Managers of the Archæological and Palæontological Department of the University of Pennsylvania. It had been decided to make further investigation by surveying and digging. Mr. Mercer, during an exploration authorized by that Board, discovered the group of pits near Macungie, and then was told of the other group.

In answer to inquiries, President Brinton said that black chert arrow-heads were found on the Susquehanna, but none on the Delaware. The Algonquins on the Delaware used jasper and quartzite for arrow-heads, but apparently not the black chert. Arrow-making was not a special trade among the Indians, but an accomplishment of every man; yet some few in a tribe were particularly expert.

Dr. R. H. Lamborn exhibited a finely-wrought copper turtle, unusually large, about three inches in diameter, found in digging a post-hole for the foundation of a house at Casa Grande, Chihuahua, Mexico. It had been sold by a boarding-house keeper to a dealer in Boston, who communicated it to Mr. Geo. F. Kunz, of Tiffany & Co.'s, New York. It appears as if formed of wires wound in various directions and soldered together; but, on testing, it proves to have no solder. The appearance is the result of traditionary conventionalism that persisted even after casting had been invented. A model was made with a wire, and a wax mold formed therefrom. It is said that the method of making such objects is described in Sahagun's unpublished *History of Mexico*, written in Nahuatl, in twelve books, of which President Brinton exhibited a manuscript copy of the first book at our meeting of December 4th, 1890. Dr. Gill, the zoölogist, says the copper turtle resembles the Mexican fresh-water terrapins.

Dr. Lamborn also exhibited a copper terrapin about three-quarters of an inch long, from the Chiriqui Coast, sent by Mrs. Zelia Nuttall from Europe. It is a solid casting.

He estimated the age of these objects to be perhaps five hundred to one thousand years.

President Brinton spoke of the method of making ornaments of gold wire by the Indians of Colombia, South America.

A bronze medal given by the Wyoming Historical and Geological Society, in commemoration of the Wyoming massacre, and a bronze medal, the gift of Dr. Samuel A. Green, Corresponding Member, and the same medal as the one received by meritorious students at the South from the Peabody Education Fund, were both examined with much interest.

The Publication Committee reported the completion of the publication of the Proceedings of the Society for 1890-91.

NOVEMBER 3D, 1892.

The deaths of Messrs. William Herbage, September 19th, 1891 ; Attilio Portioli, October 21st, 1891, and Jeremiah Colburn, December 30th, 1891, were announced, all Corresponding Members.

The president, Dr. D. G. Brinton, spoke on the "Symbolism of the Iroquois:"

He regretted that he could not make his communication in perfectly scientific form, on account of a promise of secrecy that had been exacted by the lady who gave him the information. He hoped, however, the injunction of secrecy would be removed before next spring. Last winter he had met two Iroquois, a brother and sister, with whom he had talked of his publication of Algonquin symbols. They then showed him some Iroquois symbols. The symbolism is aided by a rough script of the same source and of much the same character as the Algonquin script. There is a secret society among the pagan Iroquois that uses and preserves these symbols and script.

One record was a stick about four feet long, like a broom stick split in two, upon the flat surface of which was written the record or history of an important personage after his death. It begins with reciting that all the Six Nations (originally Five, as the Tuscaroras are not fully acknowledged to belong to them) have come together to celebrate the funeral of a deceased brother. The latter half of the record, in a different strain, accompanied the soul of the deceased after departure from the body, the first few days, and so on, until finally its arrival at its ultimate destination. Dr. Brinton had urged his informants to have all this record, that corresponds so closely with the Egyptian Book of the Dead, written out in full in the Iroquois language. They promised that the recommendation should be brought before the annual meeting, and it will probably be sanctioned.

Each man has a badge indicating his degree of initiation in the society. The badge is worn on his body, and is now made of metal, but was originally of shell or wood. Every mark on the badge has a definite meaning. Several exhibited were all of the lowest degree. One was shown to Dr. Brinton that was of the third degree, a gorget. It could not even be lent to him, but he made a sketch of it from memory. Anybody who understands the badges of the highest degree understands all. This badge of the third degree has two hearts superposed, the lower one reversed. The two hearts represent the dual reciprocal principles of nature; and the fundamental idea is evolution from sexual conjunction. One part of the marking of the badge is a conventional representation of the male organ; another part shows the two mammæ of the woman, with an open space representing the female organ.

It is, however, not to be supposed that the Iroquois use such emblems out of gross and lascivious feelings and habits. On the contrary, the Iroquois are extremely chaste, excelling all other Indians in that respect. Indeed, their delicacy in regard to these symbols is so great that no woman not yet past the age of child-bearing is allowed to belong to this secret order. Furthermore, one of the principal sacred rites of the Iroquois is the sacrifice of a white dog by a young man of about twenty years of age who must be of virgin purity.

Dr. Brinton pointed out a remarkable coincidence between the form of the badge he had sketched and a figure given in the Zeitschrift für Ethnologic, Part III, 1892, representing symbols of precisely the same character, in a carved wooden charm for "house protection," in the Kéi Islands. These symbols of aboriginal worship and of the dual principles are there superimposed upon Hindoo and Mohammedan symbols or words. The coincidence is perfect, showing how the same ideas find closely similar expression in widely separated and totally disconnected portions of the human race.

Mr. Westcott Bailey spoke of a similar symbol, called the "Shakespeare heart," incurved; also called the "Mary Stuart brooch," with a bow-knot over the heart.

Dr. R. H. Lamborn exhibited an ancient ring, of about the

first century of our era, dug up within a few years among the
Roman ruins. It is set with a paste gem resembling garnet,
and representing the head of Medusa. Though bought for
genuine, it was found on testing to be of paste, yet a very hard
paste that will cut glass. The garnet paste is probably a silicate
of alumina colored by cassius. Paste gems were seldom polished
on the interior of a ring, and roughness of the interior is the first
ground for the suspicion that it is paste. The setting is antique;
not of solid gold, but bronze gilded.

Mr. Abbott exhibited a coin of the Emperor Valentinian II, of
Constantinople.

DECEMBER 1ST, 1892.

Mr. Francis Jordan, Jr., Vice-President of the Society, read
a paper on his investigations near Betterton, Md., and exhibited a
large number of Indian relics, stone arrow-heads, hammers, and
other objects and fragments of pottery; all, however, only a small
part of what he had found and brought away from the Still Pond
Creek shell heap.

Mr. Chas. Henry Hart spoke of a newly-discovered original
miniature portrait of Washington by John Ramage, referred to
in Washington's diary under the date of October 3d, 1789. Mr.
Hart had already, in an article in the *Century Magazine*, May,
1890, spoken of the Ramage full-face portrait belonging to Mrs.
Moses S. Beach, of Peekskill, who obtained it in Montreal from a
lady who said the artist had given it to her father.* A month
ago, however, a gentleman from Virgina brought Mr. Hart a
three-quarters to left miniature of Washington that is also evidently by Ramage, and appears to be the genuine portrait mentioned in the diary as painted "for Mrs. Washington." It was
given by Mrs. Washington to her sister-in-law, Betty Washington
(Mrs. Lewis), and by her to her granddaughter, Mrs Otwayanna
Carter, wife of Dr. William Owen, of Lynchburg, Va., and she
gave it to Mrs. Stabler, Dr. Owen's niece and adopted daughter,
the mother of the gentleman who brought it. Mr. Hart exhibited
a photograph of it one-third larger than the original, and pointed
out that it was somewhat like the Savage picture. The Houston
engraving for Condie's *Philadelphia Monthly Magazine* for May,

---

*See also *McClure's Magazine*, for February, 1897, Vol. VIII, p. 298.

1708, is evidently from the genuine Ramage portrait, and not, as had formerly been supposed, a bad copy of the Savage picture.

On further discussion, Mr. Hart said that Mr. John Ramage was an Irishman who came to Boston just before the Revolution began, and was appointed Second Lieutenant, and after the war broke out went to Halifax with other loyalists. He afterwards came to New York, and became Second Lieutenant in a loyalist company there. He painted miniatures, and was gay in society. He fell into financial difficulties through endorsing the notes of friends. He removed to Canada in 1794, and there he painted portraits again. He died there October 24th, 1802, and was buried in the Protestant cemetery, now Dufferin Square. He made a claim for land bounties from the British Government and received something. His son lives at Orange, N. J., and has several relics of his father's furniture.

Mr. Maxwell Sommerville, reminded by the frame of the Ramage miniature, spoke of a certain onyx portrait in his collection with a somewhat similar soft gold frame, dating from 1492.

Mr. Sommerville spoke also of a stone resembling the foot and ankle of a lame man, a natural boulder found in the sea near Cape Hatteras.*

Mr. Sommerville exhibited a Christian ring of virgin gold, supposed to be of the third century, with a cross, and the embodiment of simplicity. It had been obtained by Mr. Sommerville from the curé of Afragola, near Cuma, now of Pozzuoli.

Mr. F. D. Langenheim spoke of a shinplaster of 1814.

Mr. Cornelius Stevenson, on the part of Dr. R. H. Lamborn, presented a box of seventeen medals and badges, including the Columbian Exhibition Medal, and mostly souvenirs of the four hundredth anniversary of Columbus's discovery of America.

Mr. Stewart Culin, the Recording Secretary, was authorized to send the Society's display of American paper money, now at Madrid, to the Chicago World's Fair of next year, with their present mounting.

---

*Such natural stones are frequently found in American archæological collections, and designated as "lasts for moccasins."—S. C.

JANUARY 5TH.

The death of Mr. Alfred G. Baker, a Resident Member, was announced, December 20th, 1892.

The President, Dr. D. G. Brinton, spoke of the Historico-American Exhibition at Madrid, which he had just visited as United States Commissioner. The Exhibition was intended to illustrate the condition of America at about the time of its discovery; and there was another exhibition at the same time to show the condition of Europe from the middle of the 15th to the middle of the 18th century. Almost every country was invited by Spain to send ethnological collections to the Exhibition, and nearly every American government responded, except Canada. The United States government sent a collection; and so did the National Museum, the Peabody Institute, the Academy of Natural Sciences, and our Society. This Society's collection was well placed and well displayed, and attracted much attention. There was an exceedingly good collection from Costa Rica, and it was the first time it had ever been displayed. There were also collections from South America. Altogether, the Historico-American Exhibition filled thirty large rooms. But the season was not propitious. The building was new, not well heated nor well lighted. The weather was very cold at night. The collections will, in large measure, be carried to the Chicago World's Fair, but not all of them. They formed a very excellent series, illustrating American ethnology and history. There were also the collections of the European Exhibition to illustrate the state of civilization of Europe at the time of the discovery of America. The Spanish Government has been liberal in regard to these exhibitions. The exhibitions were originally intended to be closed with the end of December; but, after all, are now to continue through the month of January. Our Philadelphia collections, however, will be packed up and brought back this month, in accordance with the original plan, as the American delegates had no authority to extend the time. The time for exhibiting the other collections was extended one month at almost the last moment.

Mr. F. D. Langenheim spoke of a six-dollar Brunswick silver coin.

In compliance with the American Philosophical Society's invitation to send a delegate to that Society's celebration of its one hundred and fiftieth anniversary, next May, Vice-President Jordan was by vote appointed delegate to represent our Society; President Brinton having declined such an appointment, on account of being one of the American Philosophical Society's Committee for that celebration.

FEBRUARY 2D, 1893.

Mr. John T. Morris exhibited a stone, three or four inches across and perhaps half an inch thick, that he had picked up at the tombs of Assasseef, at Thebes, and had painted upon with water colors. The water had immediately sunk into the fine, slightly yellowish nummulitic limestone, leaving the very brilliant colors upon the surface. For comparison, a piece of exactly similar stone with ancient colors at the bottom of sharply-cut grooves was likewise exhibited, showing precisely the same effect and that the ancient colors had no doubt been applied in the same way.

The President, Dr. D. G. Brinton, spoke of some points suggested by the piece of ancient Egyptian carved stone that had just been exhibited Mr. Jos. D. McGuire, of the National Museum at Washington, had lately shown Dr. Brinton some results of his researches as to primitive methods of carving stone and their bearings on old Egyptian work as well as on the work of the American aborigines. In Egypt, there were two entirely different processes. In the old dynasties, from the third or fourth to the twelfth, hard granite was finely wrought; but in the later dynasties, say the eighteenth or nineteenth, or later ones, limestone was worked. The occasion of the change of material was the discovery of the use of metals, that led to the use of softer stones. The hard stones of the earlier dynasties were carved with stone chisels. The stone chisel of the same material as the statue is worked by percussion, as shown in ancient pictures of workmen at work, striking one chisel with another. The cutting chisel wears away only half as much as the stone that is carved; so that a groove can be cut or a surface polished with a stone chisel of the same material. Hence, the age of Egyptian works of art can be defined by the material. With the older, harder materials, the limbs of a statue are joined to the main body; and the arms, for example, or the hair is cut according to the requirements of the material and tools, and not necessarily in the fashion of the living subject. The statues of the third, fourth and fifth dynasties are not of soft stones. The present specimen, with its somewhat undercut grooves, was evidently made with a metallic chisel; and Dr. Brinton was confident from that fact alone that it belonged to one of the later dynasties.

Mr. Franklin Platt asked if gems were not used for cutting stones in Egypt.

President Brinton answered that Flinders-Petrie had claimed that the ancient Egyptians used saws of hard gems. But Mr. McGuire declared that every cut instanced by Petrie could be explained by a saw, so to speak, of a single tooth, such as Dr. Brinton had himself seen. But Dr. Brinton did not feel competent to decide the question.

Mr. Morris said he saw near Memphis, in a small room, a priest's tomb, 4,500 years old, the picture of a man making a chair, and sawing wood with a hand-saw. The temple was one of the oldest buildings in Egypt, but was in perfect condition in 1882.

Vice-President Jordan inquired whether the stone of the Pyramids was worked in the method indicated by Mr. McGuire.

President Brinton said that Mr. McGuire declared it was worked in exactly the same method. Mr. McGuire had in sixty-four hours made an axe of American jade, and had imitated old American work. For example, he closely copied a Mexican calendar in similar stone, in twelve to fifteen hours, with merely stone implements. Indeed, considering the little time required, it seemed now surprising that we do not find more such old works of art.

In answer to Mr. Milne's inquiry as to American jade, President Brinton said that it was found in the Tehuantepec Isthmus, in the north of British Columbia and in Alaska. There is said to be a mountain of jade in Alaska, in a very inhospitable region.

midway between the Yukon River and the Arctic Ocean, but the precise situation is not known within fifty or sixty miles, except that it is well known to the Indians. The locality is less worked now than formerly. American jade is not the same as the Chinese. The best of the so-called Chinese jade, however, comes from Burma. The appearance is different in jade from different places. Prof. F. W. Putnam believes that South American jade comes from China. But it is temerity to say by the color whence the jade comes.

A member mentioned that a Chinaman in Hongkong, wishing to sell a small jade ornament to an American tourist, yet refused to bore a hole through it, and so the purchase fell through.

Mr. Maxwell Sommerville explained that the dust from cutting jade forms a thick paste that hinders the cutting, so that jade-cutting is not liked.

President Brinton added, in answer to Mr. Platt, that the jade of Burma did not come from the ruby locality, and that the jade mines were let by the government for £60,000 a year, and the amount of jade to be taken out was limited.

Mr. Bailey said that the Chinese bored even diamonds.

President Brinton said that Mr. McGuire had also studied aboriginal drilling, and had found that he could get 320 revolutions a minute with simple apparatus. That enabled him to bore rock crystals and diorite, and especially fast when water was thrown in. Mr. McGuire fastened the aboriginal stone drill to the end of a small shaft. The point was maintained remarkably well.

Mr. Bailey described the method by which a certain jade bracelet, bought of a Chinaman in San Francisco, was forced over the hand upon a lady's wrist, so that it was seemingly impossible that it could fall off. Yet one day, in Washington, D. C., it did fall off and broke on a stone floor. She said that something must have happened to Mr. ——; and it turned out that he had that day committed suicide at San Francisco.

President Brinton spoke of the fluted stone axes from Northern Wisconsin and from Western Africa; and said he had lately seen at the Madrid Exhibition closely similar fluted axes from Uruguay. It was an instance of identical methods quite independently invented and used in widely distant parts of the world.

Mr. Sommerville exhibited a coin from Jerusalem, a "widow's mite," obtained from Mr. Sears Merrill, the U. S. Consul there, so long the American representative and so much liked. The coin was one of John Hyrcanus, 135-106 B. C., bearing cornucopiæ and an old Hebrew letter, and was very well preserved and fresh looking.

Mr. Morris exhibited a long curved sword that a German brought some years ago to a certain works in this city to be cut up into carving knives. But new steel was used instead, and the old rusty sword was thrown aside and neglected. After some years, when a sword was wanted for some amateur theatricals, it was looked up again, and on examination proved to be very handsomely etched, with the names of several campaigns in English: "Peninsula; Egypt; Waterloo; XI L. D." (11th Light Dragoons).

March 2D, 1893.

Mr. Culin resumed his duties as Recording Secretary.

The President, Dr. D. G. Brinton, read a paper on "The Aubin Collection of Mexicana," in which he stated that this remarkable collection of documents relating to the early history of Mexico was about to be made accessible to scholars by being placed in the National Library at Paris.

Mr. Maxwell Sommerville, at the special invitation of the Society, exhibited and described a collection of amulets and talismans recently acquired by him. Among them was a series of Persian talismans, one in the form of a small iron horseshoe with Arabic inscriptions. The talisman was consulted in times of danger by being placed among hot embers, and the answer was inferred from the characters that the fire made most prominent or distinct. The Arabic talismans of fine gold exhibited were of great beauty. They bear the usual Mohammedan formulæ, and one, a talismanic ring, had the names of the four archangels inscribed on a central tablet. A metal plaque, with two sets of metal dice, was also used in a kind of divination.*

Mr. Sommerville also exhibited a small wooden image, such as are usually described as idols, from the Congo. A piece of mirror set in its breast was explained by him as due to the belief among the natives of the Congo that the monsters or spirits

---

*See Report. U. S. National Museum, for 1896, pp. 825, 826.

against which the object was used as a protection could not bear to see their own hideous visages, and hence the potency of the charm.

Mr. Culin exhibited a copy in water colors of a sheet of playing cards now in the archives of the Indies, at Seville, Spain. They were made in Mexico in 1583. Their reverses, of which a photograph was shown, are ornamented with pictures of Mexican gods and historical personages. These cards will form part of the exhibit of games to be displayed by the Museum of Archæology of the University of Pennsylvania at the Columbian Exposition at Chicago.

The question was raised as to whether the cards were made in Mexico or in Spain. President Brinton said they were undoubtedly made in Mexico. Their engraving was characteristic of Mexico, where a school of wood-engraving existed as early as 1550, of which he had many illustrations in his own library.

Mr Westcott Bailey exhibited a silver medal of Arnold Winkelried, struck in commemoration of the National Schützenfest in Nidwalden in 1861.

Mr. Culin, who represented the Society at the Historico-American Exhibition at Madrid, reported that its collections of American paper money and medals had been exhibited in connection with those of the United States National Museum at Washington, and had attracted much attention. An award of a silver medal was made to the Society for its exhibit by the Spanish Government. The collection consisted of Colonial and Continental paper money, State bank notes, private notes and postal currency, and medals of Washington, Franklin, and other eminent Americans. The combined collection of American paper money of the United States National Museum, the Antiquarian Society, and the Bureau of Engraving and Printing, displayed at Madrid is said to be the best ever made, and presented a striking exposition of the financial history of our Republic.

Mr. Charles Eyre, of Florence, Italy, presented to the Society an ancient florin from the walls of Florence. This interesting coin was obtained by Mr. Eyre some years ago when the ancient walls of the city were torn down. It fell from the ruins and was obtained by Mr. Eyre from a workman.

Mr. Culin presented an uncirculated Spanish dollar of the year 1776. It was one of twenty similar pieces paid into the Madrid office of the Equitable Life Insurance Company of New York by one of its policy holders.

March 24th, 1893.

A project for a change of quarters for the Society was discussed at a special meeting, but final decision was postponed.

April 6th, 1893.

Professor Maxwell Sommerville read a paper on "Phallic Emblems," which he illustrated with an interesting series of objects from his private collection, some of them antique bronzes.

Mr. Stewart Culin read a paper entitled, "A Day at Perugia," * in which he gave an account of Prof. Bellucci's collection of amulets.

Mr. Francis C. Macauley presented a coin of the Duke of Burgundy; and Mr. Culin, the Columbus medals of Genoa and Barcelona.

May 4th, 1893.

Mr. Lyman was requested to act as Recording Secretary during Mr. Culin's absence at the Chicago World's Fair.

The death was announced of Hippolite Taine, Corresponding Member, on March 5th, 1893; and of Right Rev. Wm. Ingraham Kip, Honorary Vice-President for California, April 6th, 1893.

Mr. W. Bailey spoke of an 1804 dollar, of which Mr. Brick, collector, of Arch Street, above Eighteenth, had said that he would not sell it for $1,500, and that he had refused $1,000 for it. It had belonged to Mr. Brick's grandfather.

The President, Dr. D. G. Brinton, spoke of the antiquity of man in America, as indicated by any implements used by him, and called it at present a very burning question. The matter had been brought up in connection with the so-called paleolithic implements that Dr. C. C. Abbott had described at one of our meetings, some years ago, as occurring in the Trenton (N. J.) gravel. Dr. Abbott's position has been criticized, but he still maintains that man existed at Trenton when the great glacier came within sixty miles of that city. On the other hand, the Bureau of Ethnology at Washington insists that man did not

*Published in Putnam's *Historical Magazine*, October-November, 1893.

live hereabouts when the glacier was there; and doubts whether any human race existed in America previous to the recent Indian ones; and declares that there is at least no proof of such a fact, though not denying its possibility. The matter has now become almost a personal one. Prof. F. W. Putnam, of the Peabody Museum, Cambridge, sides with Dr. Abbott. But there is an extreme difference of opinion between men who have made a specialty of such matters for many years. Hence, we must not decide too hastily; and Dr. Brinton's own opinion is that the question is still an open one; that there is no proof yet that man existed during the glacial period, though no proof to the contrary. For the past six months it has been the great question in Americanism; not only a personal one, but, unhappily, a local one. South of Philadelphia there are no believers in the existence of man during the glacial period; all the believers in glacial man are north of Philadelphia. Dr. Brinton had previously exhibited supposed paleolithic implements; the Washington men, however, say that they are not paleolithic implements but only rejects, incomplete attempts at implements. The question is not yet at all settled. But without reference to tools, for indirect physiological reasons, man must have existed here very long ago.

The bronze medal of the Columbian celebration in Spain was announced as received from the Spanish Government within the past few days, and was exhibited to the meeting. On motion of Mr. Milne, the President was requested to write a suitable acknowledgment of the medal, with appreciation of the praiseworthy part the Spanish Government had taken in the celebration of Columbus's discovery.

Mr. Bailey spoke of a very fine Columbus medal that had been struck in Milan, Italy, and offered for sale.

Mr. F. D. Langenheim, Curator of Numismatics, exhibited two Columbian medals, one of the Gorham Manufacturing Company.

Mr. Milne inquired if there were a catalogue of the coins and medals belonging to the Society. President Brinton answered that one had been made.

OCTOBER 5TH, 1893.

The death was announced of Mr. Anthony J. Drexel, June 30th, 1893; and of Mr. Samuel Baugh, at the age of over 82 years, August 27th, 1893; both Resident Members.

The President, Dr. D. G. Brinton, spoke of the alleged aboriginal inscriptions found in the eastern United States; and in particular of a certain piece of slate from eastern Long Island, inscribed on both sides, of which a plaster cast had been sent to him for examination. The inscription on one side was too indistinct to be traced; the other was traced, and exhibited a supposed pictograph. A number of inscribed tablets had been found in the Mississippi Valley, at Davenport, Cincinnati, and elsewhere. There were also the Lenape stone, described in Mr. Henry C. Mercer's book; and the inscribed shell of Claymont, Delaware; both with the picture of a mastodon.

Hitherto no criterion had been laid down for judging properly of such inscriptions, and various opinions have been held about them. Now there is such a criterion; for certain tribes did have a method of writing that is seen to be governed by definite principles. The characters used were: 1st, A true picture of an object; for example, a deer, a man, a wolf. 2d, Symbolic writing, such as the paw of a wolf, the three toes of a turkey; taking only a part of the whole within the original concept. 3d, Emblematic writing; taking something in the animal, and a part for the whole, but only in an allusive way; as, for instance, a medicine man is represented by a mallet, or the instrument the medicine man strikes his drum with.

Those three principles exhausted the pictographic method, with no exception. In the Indian pictography, every single picture is taken by itself alone; and there is never anything like composition, or a combination of several pictures of single objects into a landscape. In Mexico, to be sure, composition is found; but never east of the Mississippi. Here every picture of an object is separate, and stands by itself, like a Chinese character. In a row of figures each one is separate. That fact is overlooked by imitators. There are no pictures of events composed. Later, however, when Indians have learned in school, they do make compositions, but not before. By this criterion many such writings are known to be false.

This one from eastern Long Island has at the top the figure of a man, next a canoe, then an animal, a bow, a cross, a figure not yet understood, a fish, a serpent, a house or tepee with the centre-pole and others against it. If not genuine, it is a good imitation. It may possibly be a record of an Indian going on a hunting expedition and killing certain animals. It is not impossibly, and even not improbably, the record of a hunting expedition. It is not in the style of a medicine-writing.

President Brinton added that he had sent, this summer, for photographs of the inscriptions at Chattauta, East Tennessee. They are evidently natural markings, geological in character, formed of fine-grained sandstone, upheaved, and with natural shrinkage cracks that might be mistaken for writing, but only natural and geological.

Many such false or fraudulent inscriptions are coming up from time to time, two or three every year; but they can be detected by means of these principles.

Vice-President Jordan asked if there were any decipherment of the inscriptions.

President Brinton answered that some marks, foot-prints, had explanatory legends or traditions. Some were considered to be tracks of gods. Some such inscriptions at Newark have been considered to be records of the Shawnees when they removed to the West.

Mr. Jordan asked if any pictographs described the flood.

President Brinton answered that none did, except some in Mexico, one of which, a celebrated one, he described as it was in a Mexican codex, pictured and described by Humboldt.

In answer to an inquiry by the President, Mr. Platt said that the only instance of a native inscription in Mashonaland, given in Bent's book, may be explained by natural fissures in the sandstone.

Mr. Jordan inquired about the Susquehanna pictographs.

President Brinton answered that in California inscriptions carefully and laboriously painted or cut, with much time and trouble, sometimes have been made only for very temporary purposes,—telling, for example, where the tribe is going on an expedition. Sometimes inscriptions are made with enormous pains. There is an inscription at Apuru, on the Orinoco, that must have been made by men let down with ropes from the top of a high cliff. It must have been made for ceremonial purposes. The makers are unknown.

Mr. Platt spoke of the cuneiform inscriptions on the banks of the Euphrates. But Dr. Brinton said they were not hieroglyphic or pictorial; though the oldest cuneiform has been argued to be a development of pictography. Yet the oldest is still in the same wedge-shaped form as the later. De la Couperie's theory

4

was also mentioned, identifying the Accadian oldest forms with Chinese; but Dr. Brinton pointed out that Halévy, Haupt, and some others regarded the oldest Accadian as merely a hieratic script and really a Semitic language, Babylonian, with characters of different phonetic values and with terminations; though others claim it to be Turanian,—a question not yet decided.

Special thanks were voted to Mr. Clarence B. Moore for the three fine framed photographs of the Boro Budur Temple of Java.

President Brinton gave the Society a medal, struck and for sale at Chicago, representing the Mexican Calendar Stone.

NOVEMBER 2D, 1893.

The President, Dr. D. G. Brinton, spoke of recent archæological explorations in Asia Minor. Anatolia is one of the most interesting fields for archæological exploration. Noah is said to have landed on Ararat; and many things point to the region as a central spot in the history of mankind, whence tribes of men were dispersed. Recent important investigations have been made by Germans, Frenchmen, and Russians. In the north lived the Hittites, now called Chaldi, near Lake Van, partly in what is now Russian territory, partly in Turkish; and the most important studies of them have been made by Russians. There have also been researches by the French; for example, by Hyvernat; likewise by the English, Sayce and others. It is found that about six or seven hundred years before Christ there was a tribe there that developed a civilization of considerable importance. They had a written language, written with a syllabary. They have been identified with the Hittites of the Bible. The Egyptians, about the time of the eighteenth and nineteenth dynasties, were in constant conflict with the Hittites. But it has now, within the last year, been proved by Halévy, through their inscriptions, that the Hittites were Semitic. The latest writers, however, speak of the Vans, or Chaldi, as Pseudo-Hittites, distinct from the Bible Hittites, who were Semitic. For it is now probable that the later Hittites were Aryans; but Sayce makes them Georgians; others make them Turanians. Yet, though Aryans, they developed a separate method of writing. Half a dozen words have been made out. An inscription at Teprocalli, almost interpreted, shows that they were perhaps connected with the ancient Armenians. At

Sinjirli were found inscriptions six hundred or seven hundred years old that proved to be in the Phœnician dialect.

There is a peculiar appearance in some of the inhabitants:— small size, round heads, dark hair; a striking resemblance in the mountaineers of Anatolia to the vigorous Auvergnats. The resemblance is based on physical peculiarities, not on the language. The question is still somewhat an open one, where the wave of Aryan migration originated. Dr. Brinton's own opinion is that it originated in Europe, crossed the Bosphorus to Asia, went to Persia, thence to Hindoostan (about 2000 B. C.), and thence to Cambodia. Language and physical characters seem to prove that. The blonde character is most strongly visible in Europe, gradually disappearing eastward, until small traces only remain in the Brahmins. The language is also purer in Europe; in Lithuania the peasants use language much more like the Sanskrit than the peasants of India do. Therefore, the migration seems to have been eastward, not westward, as we have generally been taught.

President Brinton also said that the inscription from eastern Long Island discussed at the last meeting would be published in the *Archæologist*. It has led to the pointing out of an inscription in Ohio. The Ohio inscription is very dim, on a small stone about four inches long by two inches wide, without any connection between the figures. It was apparently written in play by some Indian or Indian boy; and was probably not an inscription intended to convey any idea.

Mr. W. Bailey said he had seen an imitation scarabæus, just arrived from Italy, that was very carefully made; but with a glass the paint could be detected. Yet the scarabæus was very perfectly molded and polished, as if new. It was made of terra cotta, a very good imitation.

The Curator of Numismatics, Mr. F. D. Langenheim, reported on his work and the Society's coin collections at Memorial Hall. With Mr. Dalton Dorr, of the Pennsylvania Museum there, he had gone over the coin collections exhibited, and had been at work upon them during May, June, September, and October of this year. By his recommendation, Mr. Dorr had employed Mr. Hans M. Wilder, a Dane, to identify the coins and make a list of them. Although it had been said that there were lists of the Society's coins and of the coin collections deposited in the care of the Society by the American Philosophical Society and by the

Philadelphia Library Company, no lists had been discovered
that were precise enough to identify all the individual coins of
each of the collections.

Mr. Langenheim was by vote instructed to inform Mr. Dorr
that the Society would pay its proper share of the expense of
cataloguing the coins.

At Mr. Platt's request, Mr. Langenheim reported on the condition of the Numismatic collection, and suggested that all the
remaining coins of the Society be sent to Memorial Hall for exhibition, and moved that a committee of three be appointed to
consult with the Memorial Hall authorities as to the expediency
of sending the remaining coins to Memorial Hall to be cata-
logued and exhibited. It was so voted, and the President appointed Messrs. F. D. Langenheim, H. Rogers, and C. Stevenson
as that committee. Mr. Platt spoke in favor of the removal of
the remaining coins to Memorial Hall.

At the suggestion of the Treasurer, Mr. Harry Rogers, a committee was appointed to audit his accounts. The President appointed Mr. Franklin Platt and Mr. Chas. D. Clark as that committee.

Messrs. F. Platt, W. Bailey, and C. Stevenson were appointed
a committee to report nominations for officers and standing committees at the next meeting.

DECEMBER 7TH, 1893.

The death was announced of Charles C. Jones, Jr., Esq., Honorary Vice-President of the Society for Georgia, July 19th, 1893,
aged 62.

Mr. F. D. Langenheim read a newspaper extract on wooden
money in England; that is, the wooden tallies, or checks, used
in England, and even in the Bank of England; the same kind of
tallies as those used by bakers in Philadelphia.

The President, Dr. D. G. Brinton, read and commented on an
extract from the _Jewellers' Circular_ of November 1st, 1893,
handed him by Mr. W. Bailey. It described a prehistoric
diamond mine near Winburg, in the Orange Free State, South
Africa; a shaft about thirty feet deep, covered by dry brushwood
and stone, and containing a windlass that had fallen to the bottom, tools of good iron but primitive design, and skeletons supposed to be of men seven and eight feet high, in one case with

iron fetters on the ankles. Tunneling had been driven about twenty yards in three directions to fairly rich diamond-bearing ground.

President Brinton remarked that the diamond mines were worked after the discovery of iron; and that the height indicated by the skeletons was no doubt exaggerated, as is very apt to happen, and was probably in reality five feet and a half or six feet instead of seven. He added that Bent had discovered ruins near Zimbabwe in Mashonaland, and at Ava, the present Aksum, in Abyssinia, with inscriptions in the Himyaritic language, doubtless of about 800 B. C.; and has connected these Abyssinian and Mashonaland ruins by their architectural designs and motifs, and finds that they also resemble Himyaritic ruins in Arabia. It would appear, then, that from 1200 to 800 B. C. there was a great Himyaritic kingdom that extended all the way to Mashonaland. It is one of the most interesting of recent archæological discoveries. The Queen of Sheba brought to Solomon more gold and spices than had hitherto been known. There can scarcely be a doubt that Ophir was Mashonaland, which would therefore be included in a reconstruction of the great Arabian Himyaritic kingdom.

Mr. Franklin Platt spoke further of the fact that Arabia was anciently often mentioned as the source of gold; but that Arabia itself really produces no gold. Also that in Falmouth Harbor a mold was found identical with the form of the gold ingots of Phœnicia.

President Brinton recalled that, according to the Book of Kings, Phœnician sailors were sent in the ships that went to Ophir.

Mr. Platt further pointed out that on the streams of the South African coast it was only the lower forty or fifty miles that were unhealthy, and that further up stream the country was healthy; that there were numerous ancient mining drifts, and that the alluvium of the valleys had been washed for gold, every foot from the headwaters to the ocean; that a thousand years must have been required for so much work.

Mr. Maxwell Sommerville said that judging from some inscriptions the Himyarites existed perhaps until Mahomet's time. Mahomet gave the remaining districts where the Himyaritic language was used some decades, perhaps forty years, in which they might continue to use that language. Many inscriptions were probably written in gold in the Himyaritic language as late as A. D. 600 or even 700. Mr. Sommerville promised to give the Society, at some future meeting, a photograph from Paris with a Himyaritic inscription.

Mr. Langenheim exhibited a set of Hawaiian coins, all silver, which he thought were made at the San Francisco mint.

Dr. R. H. Lamborn exhibited some Samoan fire-sticks, that he had obtained from the Samoan village at Chicago during the World's Fair; and he showed how they were used. The man who kindles the fire sits on the floor of the cabin, and one piece of the wood is laid on the floor and one end of the other stick is pressed with much muscular force upon the first, and rubbed continuously and rapidly back and forth, producing the right amount of wood-powder at the proper place, at the end of the little channel worn by the rubbing, and in half a minute igniting it by the heat of the friction. The wood of these specimens was Samoan; but they said that one kind of wood growing near Chicago would do.

Dr. Lamborn also exhibited a specimen from the lowest and best layer of the Catlinite red pipestone quarry. The stone is still used in barter by the Indians, who come in their wagons and carry it away, and have done so for three years past. The whole bed is about ten inches thick, divided into layers from half an inch to two inches thick. A piece five inches square and two inches thick is valued at $30 by the Indians. The man who sold the present specimen has land there, and has laid out a town there called Pipestone, and is about to publish a book about the place.

Dr. Lamborn furthermore spoke of a machine for immensely reducing drawings with absolute accuracy, particularly for making types; but it might also be used for making medals. For brevier type the reduction is one sixteen-thousandth of the original surface of the drawing. Purely mechanical means only are used, and the principles of the pantograph carried out with extreme care. The machine is used in making all the best type. A drawing is made, nine inches long, and then accurately reduced. Only eighteen machines have been made, costing $5,000 each. The machine was exhibited in Machinery Hall at the Chicago World's Fair.

Mr. Sommerville exhibited a small but very remarkable engraved stone, with a camel engraved on it and a Sassanide inscription, recently obtained by him through Professor Hilprecht at Constantinople. Such stones are almost all imperfect; but this one is only slightly fractured at the edges and is nearly perfect. Mr. Sommerville has seen thousands of such stones, but never before one with a camel. The stone, he said, dates from about A. D. 250.

Mr. Sommerville extolled the attainments of Dr. Isaac H. Hall, who had been drawn away from Philadelphia to the New York Metropolitan Museum. Dr. Hall reads many of the Abraxas inscriptions most remarkably, equal to anybody in the French Academy of Inscriptions. In Mr. Sommerville's book, near the end, there are a page and a half of inscriptions deciphered by Dr. Hall.

Mr. Langenheim reported for the committee on the removal of the Society's remaining coins that Mr. Dorr, of the Pennsylvania Museum, had expressed gratification at the proposal to deposit them there. Mr. Langenheim said the coins already there were properly listed and very safely exhibited. Mr. Dorr, in a letter dated the 7th of December, had urged that the whole expense of listing the 2,200 coins, or thereabouts, amounting to about $66, should be paid by the Society; though his original purpose was that the Society should pay one-half the expense. Mr. Langenheim, in answer to an inquiry, spoke in high terms of Mr. Wilder's ability in listing the coins and of the merits of his list. Mr. Langenheim said, that Mr. Henry Phillips, Jr., had told him that of the coins exhibited at Memorial Hall about three-fourths belong to the Philadelphia Library Company, about fifteen per cent. to the American Philosophical Society, and about ten per cent. to the Numismatic and Antiquarian Society.

On motion of Mr. Platt it was voted that the committee continue its work and be authorized to deposit at Memorial Hall the remaining coins and medals of the Society, including the six hundred medals, or thereabouts, exhibited by the Society at Madrid and Chicago, where it received an award.

Mr. Sommerville suggested that a receipt be taken for the coins of the Society. Mr. Langenheim said that Mr. Dorr was only willing to accept the deposit of the coins on giving a receipt, first a provisional one, and, after listing, a detailed receipt.

The auditing committee reported that they had audited the Treasurer's accounts for 1892, and had found them correct, and would report on 1893 at the next meeting, after the close of the year.

The committee on nominations reported a list of officers and standing committees, who were unanimously elected, as given at page 7.

After discussion by Messrs. F. Platt and J. T. Morris, it was, on motion of Mr. H. Rogers, voted that Messrs. Morris and Platt be a committee to ascertain whether accommodations for the Society could be obtained in the building of the Pennsylvania Museum and School of Industrial Art, at Broad and Pine Streets, and on what terms.

January 4th.

Mr Stewart Culin resumed his duties as Recording Secretary.

Mr. Henry C. Mercer read a paper on "The Prehistoric Remains Found in the Nickajack and Lookout Mountain Caves, near Chattanooga, Tenn."

The President, Dr. D. G. Brinton, and Mr. Franklin Platt discussed the paper.

February 1st.

The President. Dr. D. G. Brinton, read a communication from Mr. Henry C. Mercer, who was unavoidably absent, on "The Condition of Early Prehistoric Man in Europe," raising the question whether the remains indicate a warmer climate than the present one. French writers take an affirmative view, but Prof. Boyd Dawkins and the English archæologists disagree with them. The bones of the reindeer are found associated with those of the rhinoceros and hippopotamus in the English caves, and as those animals could not have lived together, Mr. Mercer suggested that the relics of the sub-tropical animals might have been washed into their present position in association with the arctic fauna. He does not consider the position taken by the French archæologists can be maintained.

Mr. John T. Morris exhibited a stamped plate of copper, about two feet long, painted with conventional designs of the Indians of the Northwest Coast. He had purchased it at Fort Wrangel.

The President, Dr. D. G. Brinton, said that it was one of the objects used as money by the Haidahs and other Indians of that coast, and he declared it to be an unusually large specimen.

Mr. Culin exhibited a pack of Corean playing cards, and an object from Cairo, like a puzzle, consisting of a tube of bamboo with strings of colored worsted.

An interesting discussion occurred with reference to the unusually large quantities of Phœnician glass that is now offered for sale in New York City and elsewhere. Prof. Maxwell Sommerville said that this glass displayed forms new to collectors, but was of unquestioned authenticity. In his opinion, probably some great find had been made in a subterranean cavern, and was now put on the market by the discoverers.

On motion of Mr. Harry Rogers, it was voted that the Curator of Antiquities be authorized to deposit the Society's collection of antiquities in the Archæological Museum of the University of Pennsylvania.

The committee appointed to confer with the Trustees of the Pennsylvania Museum and School of Industrial Art made their report on the proposed removal of the Society's quarters to the School of Industrial Art, at the northwest corner of Broad and Pine Streets. The use of the library rooms at the north end of the Broad Street front had been offered for our monthly meetings, with the privilege of using a large meeting-hall instead, if desired, and with the use of a room for any entertainment after the meetings, and ample wall-space in the library for our books, if our Society should contribute one hundred dollars a year and should put up the book-shelves.

A letter was also received by the President, Dr. D. G. Brinton, from Mr. Wm. Platt Pepper, President of the Museum and School, saying: "The offer made by you, as President of the Numismatic and Antiquarian Society, to contribute yearly to our institution the sum of one hundred dollars in April of each year is accepted with thanks. The use of a suitable room, heated and lighted, will be given for the monthly meetings of your Society, on the first Thursday of each month from October to May, inclusive; also wall space for erecting book-cases and shelving (similar to our own) to accommodate your books, documents, etc.; and your members and others having authority are to have access to the library for reading the books of your Society at all times when our building is open. In case the Numismatic and Antiquarian Society gives up this agreement, it is understood that the book-cases to be erected by it (corresponding with ours) shall be left in position and become the property of the School of Industrial Art. This agreement, if it meets with your approval, may be considered as beginning at this date."

The agreement so set forth was ratified by a vote of the Society and ordered to be spread upon the minutes.

A committee, consisting of Messrs. Chas. D. Clark and Cornelius Stevenson, was appointed to sell or lease the property now occupied by the Society, southeast corner of Twenty-first and Pine Streets, and at the suggestion of Mr. Caleb Milne a sale was particularly recommended.

MARCH 1st, 1894.

The death was announced of John Baird, a Resident Member, on February 13th.

Dr. John Harshberger, a visitor, on the invitation of President Brinton, made a verbal communication on the distribution of maize in America.

Mr. Cornelius Stevenson read, by appointment, the following paper on "The Cross-bow":

THE CROSS-BOW.

BY CORNELIUS STEVENSON.

The cross-bow, called in Latin *arcus balistarius* or *balista manualis*, and in French *arbalète*, was so named to distinguish it from certain larger machines called balistæ and catapultæ, which were used for battering the walls of towns with stones and lancing darts or projectiles of immense size.

It is an offensive weapon and is composed of a stock with a steel bow fixed in the extremity, and with a groove to receive the bolt. The cord is retained in its place by a nut, which is a circular disk of bone or ivory provided with two notches, one to receive the cord when strung, the other serving as a catch for the trigger. Back of this nut is a spring, by lightly pressing which the bolt is held in its place, to prevent it from falling when the cross-bow is inclined. Two clamps on each side of the stock hold the bow firmly in its place and prevent it from jarring loose. The stock is usually made of yew, or of the wood of the pear tree; but sometimes of ebony, and then it is frequently inlaid with ivory, and the bow damascened, and ornamented with tufts of silk.

The use of weapons made upon the principle of the cross-bow seems to be common to the people of all countries; but its origin can never be satisfactorily ascertained. Some writers say it is of Sicilian origin, while others ascribe its invention to the Cretans. M. Rhodios thinks it existed among the Greeks, and that they called it *gastraphetes*, because the cross-bowman rested it on the pit of the stomach.

According to Francis Grose, Verstegan attributes its introduction into England to the Saxons at the time of Hengist and Horsa, A. D. 457, but gives no authority in support of that supposition. In a print representing their landing, one of them is shown carrying the cross-bow on his shoulder; and so likewise other figures in the picture. The cross-bow is mentioned by William of Tyre in the year 1098, about the time of the first crusade; and a manuscript in the *Bibliothèque Nationale*, at Paris, of the end of the tenth century, shows, in one of its illustrations two cross-bowmen discharging their weapons against the ramparts of the town of Tyre. On the other hand, the Bayeux Tapestry, of the end of the eleventh century, shows both the Normans and Saxons armed with long bows, and it would appear that neither army used the cross-bow at that time; although some writers say that William the Conqueror employed cross-bowmen in his army at the battle of Hastings. Sir Samuel Meyrick * is clearly of the opinion that the cross-bow was in use among the Normans; for he says that "in Domesday Book mention is made of Odo the *arbalester*, as a tenant in capite of the King's lands in Yorkshire. The name shows him to have been a Norman, and this instance is sufficient to prove the introduction of the weapon ; though the smallness of the number used might occasion its not being represented in the Bayeux Tapestry." This writer also thinks that during the reign of Rufus it was used principally for hunting purposes; and Wace tells us that Henry, going the same day to New Forest, found the string of his cross-bow broken, and, taking it to a villain to be mended, saw an old woman there who told him he would be king.

The Abbé Suger, in his life of Louis VI, mentions the cross-bow as used in the beginning of the reign of that monarch, about 1108. But at the Council of Lateran, in 1139, Pope Innocent II forbade its use among Christian nations, as being "deathly and hateful to God;" but permitted it against infidels; and the prohibition was confirmed by Pope Innocent III. In spite of this interdict, however, Richard I, of England, armed a part of his army with the arbalist; and, as he was killed by a quarrel shot from one, while besieging the castle of Charlez, near Limoges, in Normandy, his death was considered as a judgment from heaven, inflicted upon him for his impiety. Philip Augustus also formed some bodies of cross-bowmen, both on foot and on horseback.

The Germans made very little use of missile-weapons, until

---

* Note at foot of page 15, Vol. I, of Meyrick's *Critical Inquiry into Armour*

the invention of the cross-bow. It seems to have been introduced in Germany at quite an early period, as is evidenced by
some frescoes in the cathedral of Brunswick, painted in the reign
of Henry the Lion, who died in 1195; and by paintings done in
the thirteenth century in the chapel of Saint John at Ghent. It
is well-known that Boleslaus, Duke of Schweidnitz, introduced
among his subjects the practice of shooting with the cross-bow
in the year 1286; and a little later it appears at Nuremberg and
Augsburg.

During the reign of James I, King of Aragon, in the thirteenth
century, the cross-bow was so elaborate and expensive a weapon
that the cross-bowman was regarded as the equal in rank of a
knight, a distinction at that time of great importance; and it was
enacted that "no knight's son who is not a knight or cross-
bowman shall sit at table with knights or their ladies."

After the revival of this arm by Richard I, it was much used
in England; and, in the list of forces raised by Edward II against
the Scots in the year 1322, the cross-bowman made the second
article in the enumeration of the different kinds of soldiers. In
the reign of Henry V, of England, the cross-bows were made
powerful enough to send the quarrels forty rods; for, in the *Dun-
stable Chronicle*, we read that "Henry V came near to the city
of Roan by forty rods of length, within shotte of quarrell."
Cross-bows were frequently used as weapons of defence and
mounted on the tops of castles, behind the crenelles of turrets
pierced to shoot through, and they were then called crenequins.

The cross-bow was also considered a royal weapon; and Gerard
de la Warre, in the reign of Henry III, was appointed cross-bow
bearer to that sovereign, and valuable manor lands granted to
him, conditional upon his providing cross-bow strings, or
materials for making them. Henry VII, however, towards the
close of his reign, forbade its use, in order to encourage the more
general use of the long bow. But there was a reservation in
favor of the nobility; for by the statute 19 Hen. VII, c. 4, A. D.
1508: "No man shall shoot with a cross-bow with the King's
license, except he be a lord, or have two hundred marks of land."
So strong was the dislike of Henry VIII to this weapon, that,
notwithstanding the statute of Henry VII, he caused another
statute to be passed in the year 1515 prohibiting its use. These
statutes do not, however, seem to have had the desired effect;
for, in less than twenty years after, their use had become so

common that a new statute was deemed necessary, which imposed a penalty of twenty pounds on anybody that kept one in
his house. Its gradual decline in England, however, may date
from that period, and no cross-bowmen are to be seen in the
paintings of the period representing the battles of Henry VIII.
This may be owing to the more general use of gunpowder and
the great improvement in the art of gunnery. The use of the
cross-bow seems to have been somewhat revived in the reign
of Queen Elizabeth, for we find that in the year 1572 the Queen,
in a treaty with King Charles IX, of France, agreed to furnish
six thousand men, armed partly with long bows and partly with
cross-bows.

Independently of the mercenary cross-bowmen, composed for
the most part of Genoese and Gascons, in the armies of France
from the thirteenth century, a great number of the large towns
of the northern provinces of that country possessed companies
of cross-bowmen. In 1230, an Act of Parliament gave the title
of Master of the *Arbalétriers* to Thibaut de Montléard. This
office was considered of great importance and next in rank to
that of Marshal of France, and in 1515 was united with that of
Grand Master of Artillery. Charles V, in 1359, established for
the defence of Paris a body of *arbalétriers* composed of two
hundred men, and they elected each year four provosts from their
fraternity, who each commanded fifty men. Each man received
in time of peace "*deux vieux gros d'argent, ou la valeur*," a day,
and double that sum when in active service, besides enjoying
numerous privileges. This body grew in number in a short time;
for, in 1375, we find it augmented by royal ordinance to eight
hundred men; and their privileges seem to have grown in pro-
portion. They were not bound to serve beyond the limits of
their district, without the consent of the Provosts of Paris and
the "*Prévosts des Marchants*"; although they frequently took the
field when the necessities of the crown were pressing.

During the reign of Charles VII, the cross-bow became so
popular that it almost superseded the long bow; and it was only
abandoned as an arm of war under the reign of Francis I. At the
battle of Marignan, in the year 1515, however, there were still
two hundred *arbalétriers* on horseback, who formed the guard of
Francis, and who rendered signal service. Père Daniel, the
author of *Discipline Militaire*, says that at Bicoque there was only
one *arbalétrier*, but so skilful was he, that "an officer, named

Jean de Cordonne, having opened the vizor of his helmet to take
breath, this man struck him in the unguarded part with his arrow
and killed him." Finally, in the year 1627, at the siege of La
Rochelle, there were some English cross-bowmen in the pay of
Richelieu who distinguished themselves at the attack on the
island of Ré.

As a missile-weapon the cross-bow was admirable, alike for the
accuracy of its aim and for the power of sending its projectiles.
Its only disadvantage was its weight and the length of time required to string the bow. For, in the fourteenth century, when
it had reached a high state of perfection, a skilful cross-bowman
could only shoot about two arrows a minute; while an archer
could send a dozen, as he had only to stoop and pick one up from
the bundle which he had placed under his foot, without taking his
eye from his enemy.

Grose cites Sir John Smith as saying, in his *Instructions and
Observations*, that the cross-bow would kill point-blank between
forty and sixty yards, and if elevated, seven or eight-score yards,
or further. The long bow, however, in the hands of a powerful
archer would carry upwards of 250 yards. William de Bellay,*
in his *Instructions for the Wars*, written in the year 1589, gives
the cross-bow a still greater range. He says: "And were it so,
that the archers and cross-bowmen could carry about with them
their provision for their bows and cross-bows as easily as the
harquebusiers may do theirs for the harquebusse, I would re-
commend them before the harquebusse, as well for their readiness
in shootinge, which is much more quicker, as also for the sure-
ness of their shot, which is almost never in vayne. And
although the harquebusier may shoote further, notwithstanding,
the archer and cross-bowman will kill at one hundred or two hundred paces off as well as the best harquebusier. And sometimes
the harnesse, except it be the better, cannot holde out. At the
uttermost the remedy is that they should be brought as neare
before they do shoote as possibly they may, and if it were so
handled, there would be more slain by their shot than by twice
as many harquebusiers. And this I will prove by one cross-bowman who was at Thurin when the Lord Marshal of Annehault
was governor there, who, as I have understood, in five or six
skirmishes did kill or hurt more of our enemies than five or

---

* Grose's *Military Antiquities*, Vol. II, note at foot of page 289.

six of the best harquebusiers did during the whole time of the siege."

In case of rain, the cord of the long bow could easily be detached and put away; while that of the cross-bow, on the contrary, was usually fixed in such a way as to remain permanently, until worn out or removed to be repaired. The rain having wet the cords of the cross-bows at the battle of Cressy (1346) had an important influence on the result of the battle. The French employed fifteen thousand Genoese cross-bowmen in their army; but the day before the battle, Froissart tells us, they were quite fatigued, having marched on foot six leagues completely armed and with their cross-bows. The Genoese were ordered to the front to begin the fray; but a heavy rain, which had fallen before the commencement of the action, had wet the cords and rendered them useless. The English archers, who, during the shower, had put their bows into their cases, withdrew them uninjured, and, taking advantage of this, shot their arrows with such force and effect that it seemed as if it snowed. "When the Genoese felt these arrows, which pierced their arms, head, and even their armor, some of them cut the strings of their bows, while others flung them on the ground, and all turned about and retreated quite discomfited. The French had a large body of men-at-arms on horseback rightly dressed to support the Genoese; but the King of France, seeing them in this disorganized condition, cried out: 'Kill me those scoundrels, for they stop up our road without any reason.' You would then have seen the above-mentioned men-at-arms lay about them, killing all they could of these runaways."

The Genoese, who were always celebrated for their skill in the use of this weapon, do not seem to have lost their prestige by reason of their ill success in this battle; for we find Charles, Earl of Blois, the next year, employed two thousand of them at the siege of La Roche de Rien; and in the *Chronicle of Bertrand de Guesclin* we read: "Seventeen thousand were armed, without reckoning the cross-bowmen, who were Genoese." And again, at the siege of Brest, Froissart tells us that "the Genoese, who were at the edge of the town ditch, and kept up a steady discharge of their arbalests, harried those of the town to such a degree that they durst not show their heads above the battlements; for the Genoese cross-bowmen are such expert marksmen that whenever they aim they are sure to hit."

PLATE II.

Num. and Antiq. Soc. Proc., 1892-98.

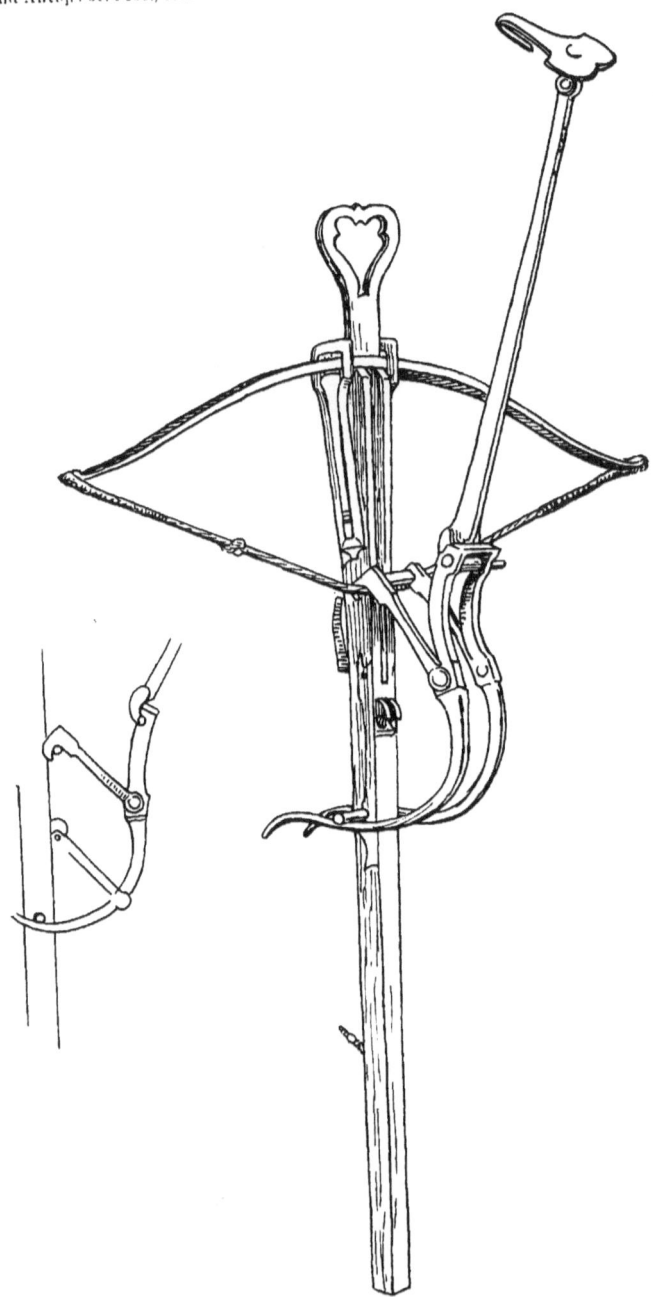

Arbalète Pied-de-biche. Author's collection.

At the commencement of the fifteenth century all the cross-bows then in use had their strings drawn by means of machinery; and of these there were three distinct varieties: the *arbalète à pied-de-biche*, or hind's foot; the *arbalète à tour*, or rolling-purchase cross-bow, sometimes called the *arcubalista grossa ad stapiam*, or great stirrup cross-bow; and the *arbalète à cry*, or *à cric*, or, in English, latch cross-bow. Although some sort of mechanism was used before this time for stringing the bow, we have no reliable information on the process employed for doing so. The manner of bending the bow by means of the foot is very old, authority being found for it by Guillaume le Breton, who wrote in the twelfth century; and the manuscript illustrations of the thirteenth and fourteenth centuries show cross-bows furnished with a stirrup and a hook fastened to the belt by a strong leather strap, which enabled the cross-bowman, by lodging the cord of the bow in the hook and leaning his weight upon his foot in the stirrup, to draw the cord slowly to the nut. But I do not think that the hind's foot cross-bow, the first of the three above named, was in use before the commencement of the fifteenth century; at least, we do not, before that epoch, find any other method of stringing the bow than the one just described. The *arbalète à tours*, or rolling-purchase cross-bow, is seen in paintings about the year 1425; and the *cric*, or latch cross-bow, the last fitted with a mechanism, and also the most powerful, made its appearance about the beginning of the sixteenth century.

The *arbalète à pied-de-biche*, or hind's foot cross-bow, was lighter than the others, and usually carried by horsemen at the saddle-bow. By means of a small stirrup at the extremity of the stock it hung suspended from a hook in the saddle. A short distance below the bow, a hook was fixed in such a manner as to attach itself to the saddle and prevent the bow from shaking and tossing about. The machinery used to bend this cross-bow is a lever, composed of two pieces. One of these pieces, the arm of the lever, is divided into two branches, each provided with a sort of fork. In bending the bow, one of these forks grasps the cord, and the other branch, by means of its long fork, rests on projecting pieces of iron on each side of the stock. The cross-bowman, seizing the lever, draws it towards him, and the fork with the cord in its grasp, following this movement, is brought into the notch, where it is held, and the bow is strung. The apparatus is then removed, and attached to the belt by a hook at the end of the lever.

The mechanism for stringing the bow was much quicker, and was less complicated, than that of the rolling-purchase cross-bow; but the bow was not so powerful, and had shorter range. This arm being light, in order to aim properly, it was not necessary to place the butt of the stock under the arm, or to steady the elbow of the left arm against the side, as was the case with the larger bow. With the larger weapon, however, the butt of the stock being placed under the arm, in order to steady it, the cross-bowman had to incline his head to aim accurately. The foot cross-bowmen acquired, however, great skill, and rarely missed their man.

The *arbalète à tours*, or rolling-purchase cross-bow, was too large and cumbersome a weapon to be carried on horseback, and was used by foot soldiers only; and during the first part of the fifteenth century was employed for the defence and in the attack of fortified places. In Germany, such cross-bows were made very large and powerful, often measuring twenty or twenty-five feet in length, and were called *rebaudequins*. They threw a bolt seven or eight feet long, and, besides, propelled stones, clay bullets and incendiary projectiles.

These formidable weapons were mounted on trunnions, and required several men to handle them, much after the manner of our modern artillery. The rolling-purchase cross-bow was long and heavy, and furnished at the end of the stock with a steel stirrup. The one in my collection is made of some very hard wood, stained a dark color and rudely inlaid with ivory. The stock measures three feet three inches in length, and the steel bow, which is fitted into the stock about four inches from the end, is about two feet four inches from end to end, two inches wide in the deepest part and nearly three-quarters of an inch thick, and the ends were so forged as to hold the loops of the cord firmly. The stirrup is six inches in length, and five inches wide at the widest part of the span. The length of the groove for the quarrel is one foot three and a half inches, including that of the nut, which is about half an inch wide. The nut is of horn, with a pivot and a steel pin to receive the extremity of the trigger, and when the bolt was shot it was reversed, having turned on its axis. The jar or concussion produced on the cord, when released from the butt in firing, was so great that it became neces-

PLATE III.

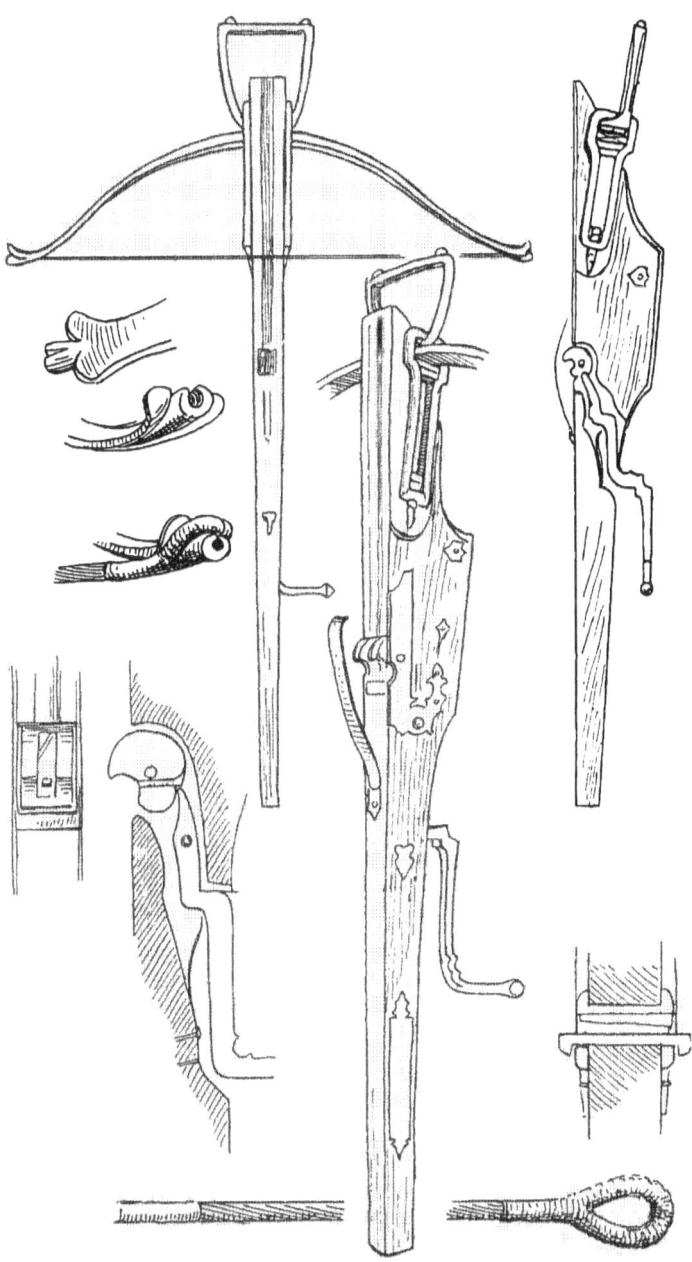

·Arbalète à tours.

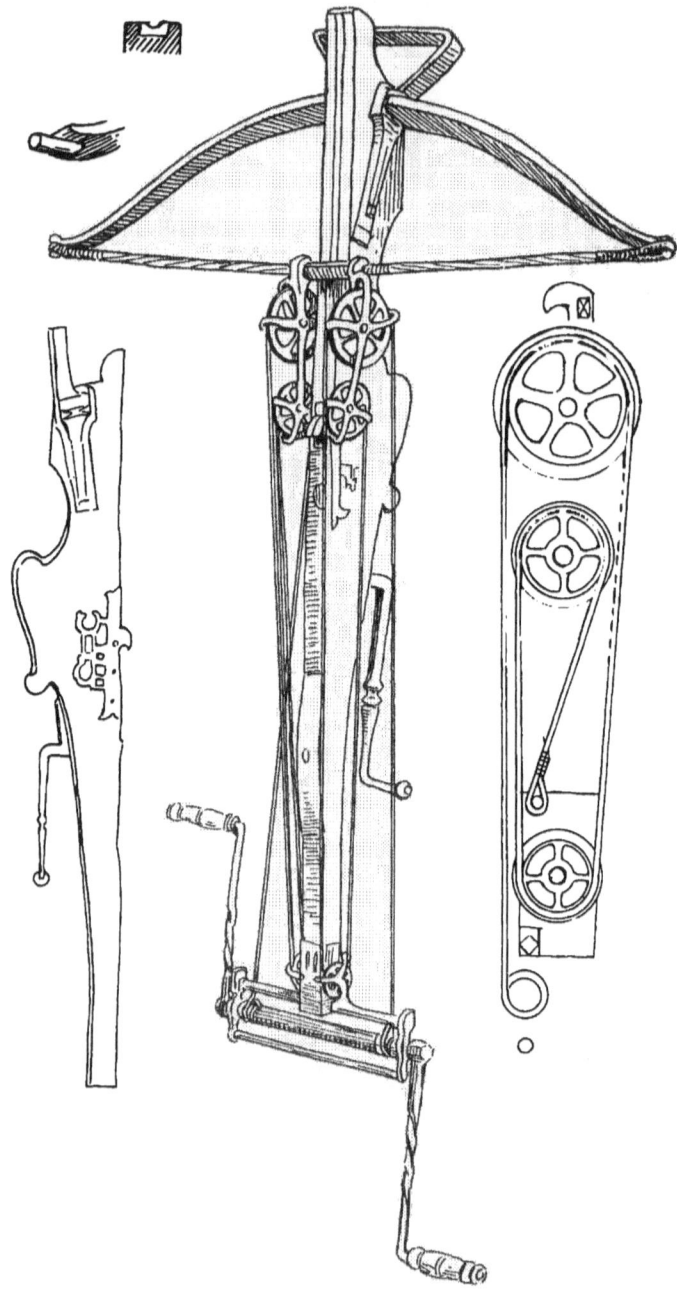

Arbalète à tours. Author's collection.

sary to fasten the bow firmly in the stock by means of two steel clamps or *renforts;* and it was frequently further protected by thick bands of rope bound over it, the wear and tear of this part of the arm being exceedingly severe. The cord itself was very thick, made usually of hemp, strongly bound round (but not twisted) at the middle and two ends.

In order to draw the cord to the nut, this cross-bow was furnished with what was called the *tour moufle,* or *moulinet,* which, after the bow had been strung, could be removed and hung at the belt, having a hook for that purpose. The *moulinet* consisted of an iron cylinder in a frame, likewise of iron, made to turn by means of two handles in opposite directions, and having a cap, also of iron, to fit on the butt end of the stock. On each side of the cap is a small pulley, the wheel of which has attached to one of its arms a cord, which passes around another wheel of equal size, returns over the first, and then goes round another wheel of double the diameter, and so passes to the cylinder of the *moulinet;* by winding which the power necessary to bend the bow is lessened to a fourth. Attached to the arms of the wheels is a claw made to slide on the plane of the stock, to catch hold of the cord and draw it to the nut.

In order to string the bow, it was necessary to place the end of the foot in the stirrup. The groove, which is of ivory, and in which the bolt rested, is slightly concave, so as to reduce the friction of the bolt on the stock. On account of the weight of this weapon, the cross-bowman, when he wished to fire, was obliged to lean the elbow of his left arm on his left side, and in that position could hold the bow firmly for several seconds.

At the commencement of the fifteenth century, we find the large pavise (or *pavois,* in French), also called mantlet, a shield so large as to be a sort of portable intrenchment, introduced for the purpose of protecting the cross-bowman from the missiles of the enemy while bending his bow. This shield was usually three feet six inches in length, and from twenty-two to twenty-four inches in width, almost entirely covering the body of the bowman. It was square in outline and convex in form, in order that missiles striking it should glide off; and also to leave a space for passing the arm when it was to be carried, or to plant it on the ground by means of a stake. The pavise was made of strips of light wood very skilfully glued together, and covered inside and out with the skin of the deer, and sometimes of the horse, or ass, and pasted with great care on the wood, which was painted or varnished over. According to Sir Samuel Rush Meyrick,* these large shields were sometimes called paniers, on account of their construction, which he describes as

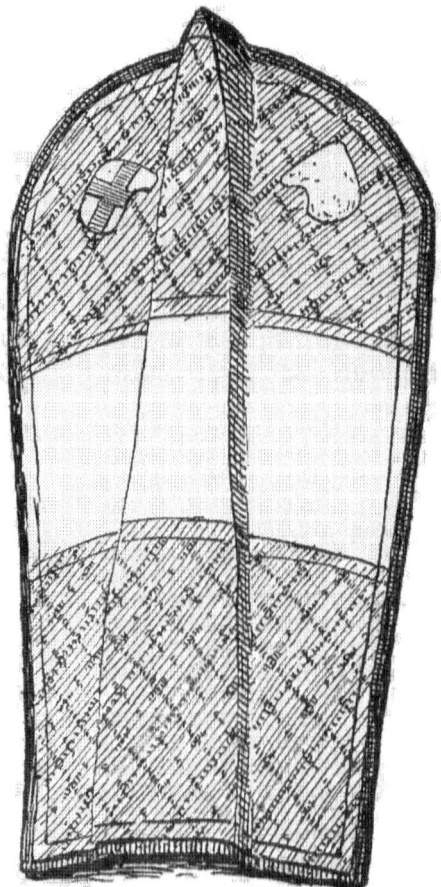

Fig. 1.—Pavise. Author's collection.

follows: "The interior was formed of osiers, over which was placed a cover of aspen wood, or black poplar, the wood of which is white and very light. Sometimes, indeed, this exterior surface was wanting, and then the osiers were more closely interwoven."

* Meyrick's *Critical Inquiry into Armour*, Vol. II, page 130.

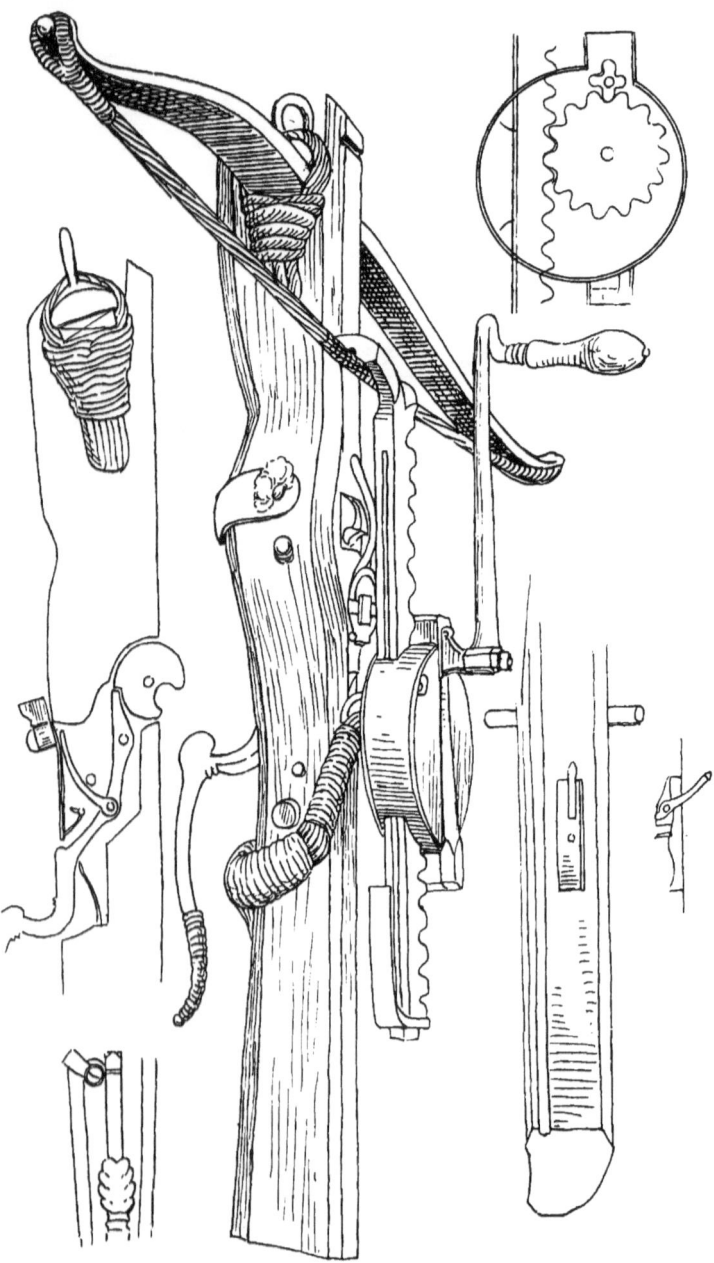

Arbalète à cric.

The shields were frequently charged with the armorial bearings of the great lord under whose banner the cross-bowman was enlisted, or of the vassal who carried them. Mr. W. H. Riggs, the Washington banker, now living in Paris, a celebrated collector of arms, has one of these rare shields; and M. Viollet-le-Duc,* speaking of it, says it is about three feet in height, and has two straps at the upper part, to suspend it on the back, and another at the lower part, through which to pass the arm. It is emblazoned with the arms of the owner on a black field : two shields, one *argent à la croix gueules*, the other *argent à la bande gueules*, accompanied by two lions rampant of the same.

Froissart speaks of the Genoese in the service of France as carrying a pavise in the shape of an elongated heart; and this form is also frequently found on the Italian monuments of the fifteenth century. Sir Samuel Meyrick thinks these shields were carried by a man who preceded the cross-bowman to defend him while he plied his shafts. M. Viollet-le-Duc, on the other hand, is of the opinion that it was habitually carried on the back, enabling him to mount with it in assaulting fortified places. It was also used for the defence of walls, and for carrying the dead and wounded from the field, a usage dating from a remote antiquity. Guillaume le Breton, in describing the siege of Roche au Moine, in the thirteenth century, speaks of a shield then in use, which he calls the "Parma," and which must have been almost identical in form with the pavise. He says the besieged, in order to get rid of a troublesome pavisor, hit upon an ingenious expedient. One of their bowmen sent forth a shaft to which was affixed a slender cord: the barb having buried itself in the Parma, he pulled the cord, overset it, and with a second shaft slew the enemy, now fully exposed to view.

Let us now turn our attention to the *arbalète à cric*, or latch cross-bow. This bow, during the hundred years or more that it was used, does not seem to have varied materially in form, and, although much shorter, and with a mechanism less complicated than either of the former, was more powerful, on account of the greater strength of the bow. The stock is short: the one in my possession measuring but twenty-three inches in length, and is three inches thick in its widest part. The bow is not held in place by clamps, as in the case of the rolling-purchase cross-bow,

---

Dictionnaire Raisonné du Mobilier Français, Vol. VI, page 217.

but by an ingenious system of stout cords wound round the bow
and run through a hole about four inches and a half from the
end of the stock.

The bow is bent by a windlass, which consists of an iron rod
with a double claw at its end and having a row of teeth the
entire length of one side. The rod passed through an iron box,
which contained a cog-wheel made to fit the teeth of the rod;
and a handle being fixed to the axle, on turning it, the rod was
advanced, until the claws grasped the bowstring; then, by re-
versing the action of the wheel, the rod was drawn back, and the
cord followed it, until it was caught in the nut, and it was wound
up. This apparatus was attached to the stock by a loop made of
strong cords, which slipped over the butt of the stock, and was
held in its place by two iron pins, which projected from each side;
and then, when the bow was bent, it could be easily removed and
hung at the belt by a hook.

This arm was carried on the back of the cross-bowman, and
was held there by a strap, which passed through a leather loop,
and from thence through a ring fastened at the upper end of the
stock. The bolt was not placed in a groove, as in the case of the
other cross-bows, but simply on a flat surface on the face of the
stock, which was of ivory, and held in place by a light spring of
horn that passed over the nut. The range of this bow is about
three hundred feet when held horizontally.

In addition to these three cross-bows, I may briefly mention
two others that were in use in the sixteenth and seventeenth centuries, but were only used in the chase: the *arbalète à jalet* (because the missiles used were stones, or lead balls) or prod; and
the *arbalète à baguette*, or barrelled cross-bow.

The first-named came into use about the middle of the sixteenth century, and was very light and graceful in form. The
stock, at about the distance of two feet six inches from the butt,
takes a curve equal in chord to the space required to string the
bow, which rendered it easy to carry on the shoulder, as well
as prevented any interruption to the projectile force of the bullet
by friction. At the commencement of this curve is placed a
small lever, which forms a hook at one end, and turns in a
movable axis. The hook is to hold the string, which, when
the lever is pushed down, is held by means of a trigger, this being
furnished with a hook to catch into a hole in the lever. The
cord is very different from the others, being double, and the

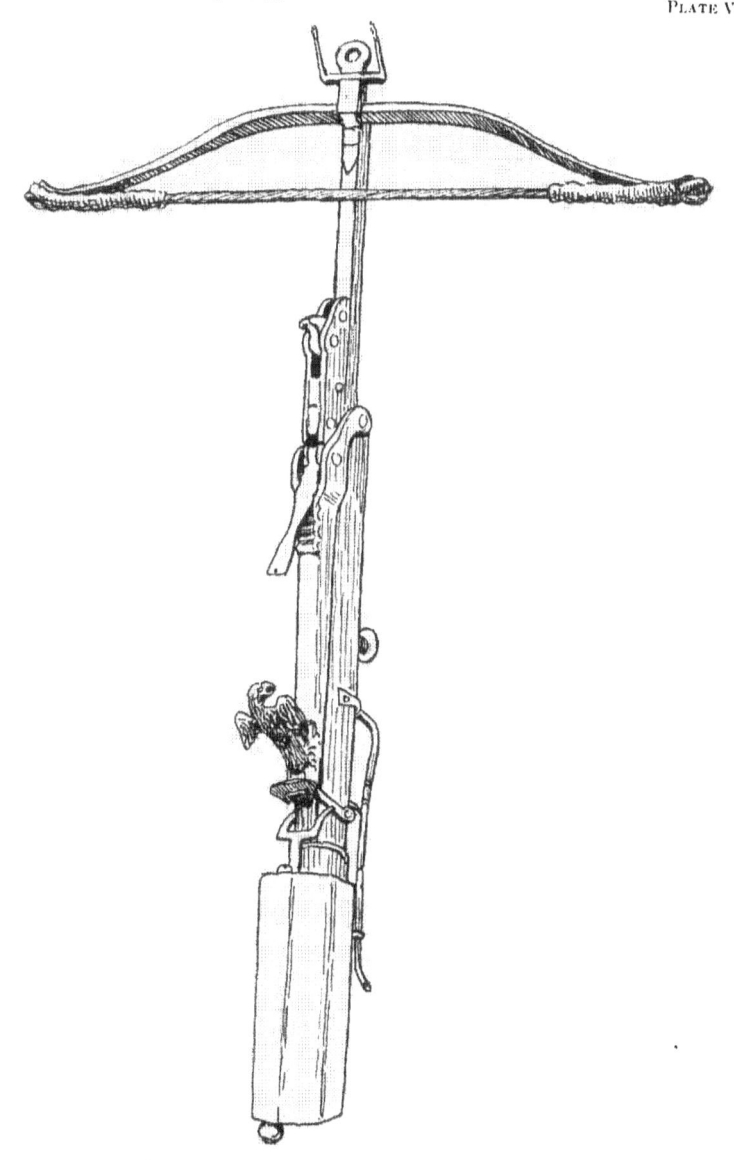

Arbalèt. à jalet. Author's collection.

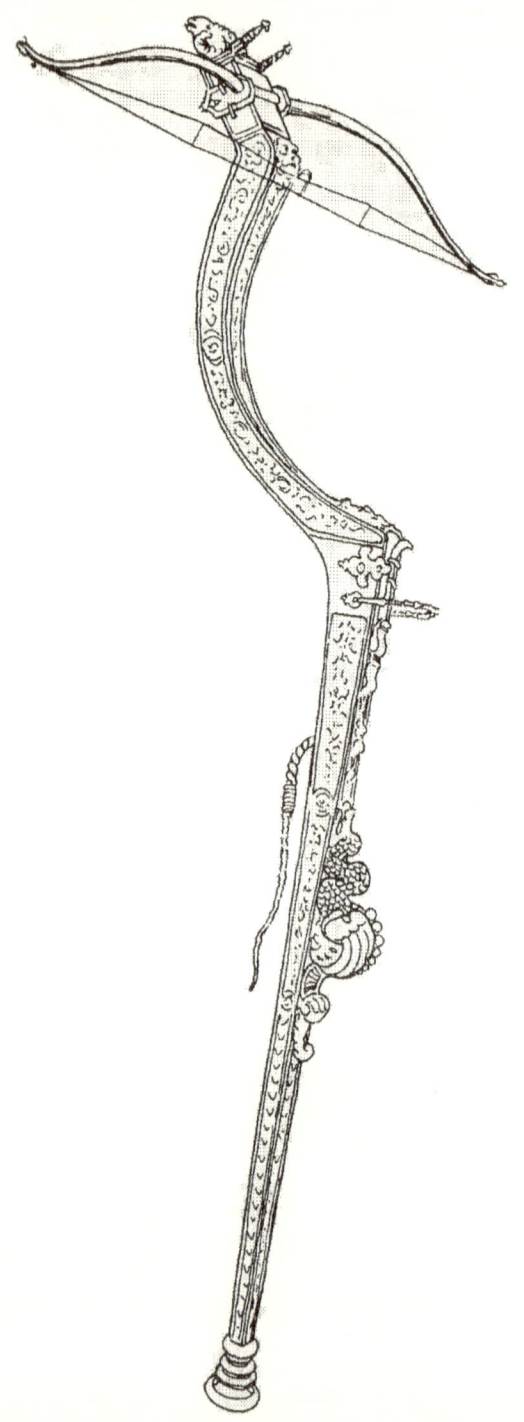

Arbalète Catherine de Médicis.   Author's collection.

two parts separated by two small cylinders of wood equidistant from the extremities and centre. These bows were often highly ornamented, and were either elaborately carved or inlaid with precious metals.

Probably the finest example existing is that of Catherine de Médicis which is preserved in the *Musée des Souverains*, form-

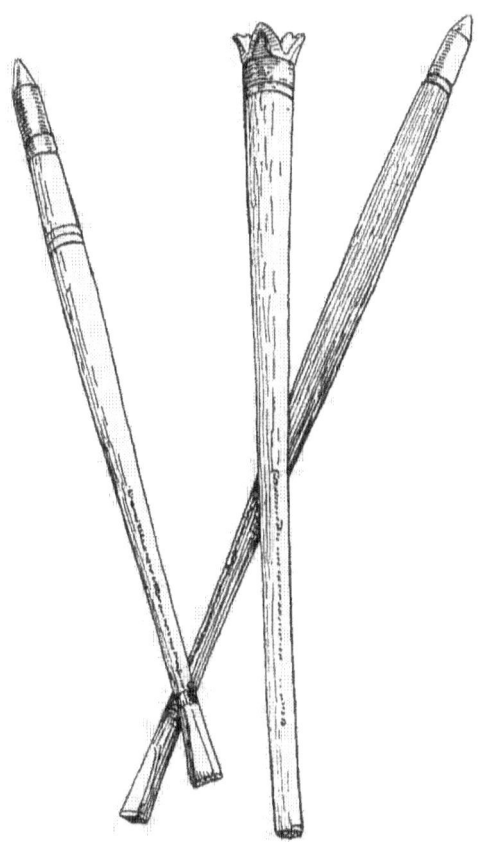

Fig. 2.—Cross-bow bolts. Author's collection.

erly in the *Bibliothèque Impériale*, Paris. It is of Italian workmanship of the best period, and the wood is yew exquisitely carved and inlaid with silver, chiseled and damascened with remarkable taste and execution. In the use of the prod Queen Elizabeth is said to have been a proficient.

The *arbalète à baguette* was an arm in use in the reign of Louis XIV, and is heavy without much strength. It is strung by means of a stick or sort of ramrod, or simply with the hand, and the groove through which the quarrel slips is covered by a half tube, leaving a passage for the string. This tube gives the stock the appearance of a gun. The projectile could either be a bolt or a bullet.

The missiles for all cross-bows (with the exception of the pebble or bullet-shooting ones) were called bolts or quarrels, from the quadrangular shape of their piles or heads. These piles or heads were very varied in form, from the square tip to the sharp, lance-like point; crescents, stars, and other odd shapes being also used. The quarrel was much shorter than the arrow, and its pile heavier and stronger; and the quarrel is only feathered on two sides, while the arrow is feathered on three. The shaft was feathered with wood, leather, or feathers, and set on straight; except with those sometimes used in France called *viretons*, which had the feathering set in a curved manner so as to regulate their flight by giving a rotary movement when passing through the air.

Another kind, called matras (or, *carreau assommeur*, in French), ended in a round knob, which killed without shedding blood. It was used in hunting, especially against feathered game, when the hunters desired to preserve their spoils uninjured. Quarrels also occasionally carried burning tow and tubes filled with inflammable material, in order to set fire to the enemy's works.

It may be of interest, before closing this paper, to speak of the equipment of the cross-bowman when fully prepared for war. It was very cumbersome and heavy. The cross-bow itself weighed about twenty pounds; the quiver, holding usually about twenty bolts, which hung attached to the belt, about four or five pounds more; while on his back he frequently carried the large pavise to protect him while he strung his bow; and at his side he carried a long sword. For headgear he wore a *chapel de fer*, or rounded helmet, but without vizor or protection for the face; and a *camail de mailles*, or collar of chain-mail, which covered the neck and a portion of the chest and shoulders. As body-armor he wore a brigantine, or sort of jacket, in the form of a doublet, the inside of which was of strong linen, or skin, and the outside of velvet, or cloth; while between these two layers of stuff were plates of steel, overlapping each other like the slats of a blind, and fastened to the outside covering by rivets, the

Fig. 3.—Cross-bowman Fully Equipped.

heads of which formed an ornament on the outside of the velvet. Under this garment he wore a hauberk, or coat of mail. *Chausses*, or leg coverings, also of linen or silk, and *genouillères*, or knee guards, protected his legs, and completed his equipment, which could not have weighed less than seventy or eighty pounds. It will be readily seen, therefore, that his proper employment was in the defence or attack of fortified places. Behind a parapet or mantelet the cross-bowman could be used to the best advantage; for, firing slowly, he should be under cover.

Prof. Maxwell Sommerville exhibited a stone carving in high relief representing the god Krishna surrounded by serpents.

Mr. John T. Morris exhibited a piece of red syenite from the unfinished obelisk at Assouan.

Mr. F. D. Langenheim exhibited specimens of early German bracteates.

Mr. G. Albert Lewis exhibited a coin struck by the Knight Templars in 1307, which had been in his family for the past two hundred years.

Mr. Tozo Takayanagi, a visitor, presented specimens of the modern paper money and silver and bronze coins of Japan, for which a special vote of thanks was passed.

APRIL 5TH, 1894.

The Society met for the first time at its new hall in the School of Industrial Art, northwest corner of Broad and Pine Streets.

The President, Dr. D. G. Brinton, made an address of welcome to the members in their new hall, and warmly expressed his personal thanks to the President and officers of the Pennsylvania Museum and School of Industrial Art for having given such fine accommodations for the Society. A formal vote of thanks to them was then passed for their hospitality.

Mr. Henry C. Mercer read by appointment a paper on the following topics: "The Arkansas Traveler";* "A Pennsylvania German Fairy Tale"; "The Blind Man and the Giant"; "Pennsylvania Counting-out Rhymes"; "Pennsylvania German Pow-wow Formulas";† "Indians Mining Lead"; "The Sunbonnet," and "The Grasshopper War."

In the discussion that followed, Mr. Culin said he believed that much of the Pennsylvania German folk-lore, particularly healing formulæ, was derived from German printed books.

A discussion also occurred on the subject of lead mining by the Indians, and President Brinton said that, as far as he knew, no museum contained any leaden object made by the natives of America previous to the Conquest. He suggested that the members of the Society while visiting foreign museums during the

---

*Published in the *Century Magazine*, for March, 1891.

†The Pennsylvania German Folk-lore was published by the author at the *Doylestown Intelligencer* press, August, 1896.

coming summer should keep a sharp look-out for such specimens.

Mr. Harry Rogers exhibited a coin of the ancient city of Philadelphia, of which he read the following account:

The ancient autonomous Greek cities invested with the right of making their own laws and coining their own money were very numerous. Among these mint cities were two of the name Philadelphia, one in Syria and the other in the kingdom of Lydia, about one hundred miles east of Smyrna and south of Constantinople. The latter city, now called Ala Shehr, one of the most important cities in Lydia, was founded by Attalus Philadelphus, of Pergamus, and was built to commemorate the love of two royal brothers. The question naturally arises here: Did Penn name the American Philadelphia after the two worthless worthies, Charles II and James II?

The mint of ancient Philadelphia is supposed to have been in operation at least some four hundred years, down to the time of the Emperor Caracalla certainly. A specimen of the work of this ancient mint having come into my possession, it seemed proper at this time to exhibit it to the Society and give a short description. The coin was struck at least two thousand years ago, and is of bronze or brass. Obverse: a female head, representing the city itself, or the inhabitants, with the word ΔΗΜΟΣ. Reverse: a running female figure, half draped, with a dog, also running, and a legend. The figure represents Artemis or Diana, who was a favorite divinity of many of the cities of Asia Minor. She has a bow with arrows and a quiver; also, the ever-present dog. The legend reads: ΦΛ ΦΙΛΑΔΕΛΦΕΩΝ ΝΕΩΚΟΡΩΝ: meaning, "Friend of the Philadelphians, Temple-sweepers,"—as one authority terms them. The last word of the legend represents all those who took care of the temples, or sextons, or vergers, as we should term them.* The coin is rare, and I know of none other in Philadelphia, save the one in the Mint collection.

Philadelphia was not far from Ephesus, where St. Paul is said to have spent much time. It was one of the seven cities of Asia Minor specially written to by St. John in the Revelation. It

---

* It is "a title found on coins, especially of Asiatic cities, assumed when they had built a temple in honor of their patron god or ruler."—*Liddell & Scott's Lexicon.*

would, therefore, seem probable that this coinage was well-known to both those apostles.

On motion of the Curator of Numismatics, Mr. F. D. Langenheim, it was voted that he be authorized to employ Mr. Hans M. Wilder to list, catalogue, and classify the Society's collection of coins and medals at Memorial Hall; that the collection remain on deposit there for five years after formal receipts for them have been given, and thereafter without expense to the Society; but that should the collection be withdrawn before the end of the five years the Society shall reimburse the Museum for the cost of the cases (about $42 each) in which the collection is exhibited; and further, that the expenses ($66.33) already incurred in listing the 2,216 specimens now on deposit be paid by the Society.

MAY 3D, 1894.

The President, Dr. D. G. Brinton, exhibited a number of Central American objects. Central America, he said, was not only central geographically, but also in point of the highest culture. Among the evidences of culture there are few which are a better index than those we find in the attempts to represent the human form and face. He then exhibited photographs of three terracotta heads from Guatemala, which bear comparison, in his estimation, with the highest creations of human art. These heads were obtained some years ago by Dr. Habel in Guatemala, and are now in the Metropolitan Museum of Art in New York City. Dr. Habel was a doctor of medicine who lived in New York some twenty years ago. After accumulating a little money in his profession, he determined to devote his life to American archæology, and went to Guatemala. His greatest find was the tablets of Santa Lucia Cozumelhualpa, now in the museum at Berlin. From Central America he went to Colombia and Peru, and while in South America was taken with a fever, and died. The three heads of the photographs were the best in his collection, and were obtained from Western Guatemala, probably, in Dr. Brinton's opinion, from Santa Lucia.

President Brinton then exhibited a perfect *fac simile* of an original American book, such as was made and printed in America before the Discovery. He used the word "printed" advisedly. Movable stamps of wood, terra-cotta, and stone were used for the purpose, but the blocks hitherto found do not contain the characters used in this book. It consists of a single long sheet, folded like a screen, exactly in the manner of the books commonly used to-day in Burma, or like many Japanese picture books. The text is on both sides of the sheet, so that, after one side has been read, the book can be turned over, and the continuation found on the reverse of the pages. The book is known as the *Codex Cortesianus*, and is a work on astrology, and appears from internal evidence to have been written about A. D. 1450. It was the first reproduction of a native American book ever made in its original book form; and was published in Madrid from the original in the Archæological Museum, at the time of the Columbian celebration in 1892. No portion of it had been translated, nor, indeed, of any other of these documents, but Dr. Brinton said he had been informed by Dr. Förstemann, of Dresden, that he would produce a translation of a whole page of a Maya manuscript at the Congress of Americanists at Stockholm. That will be the first serious attempt to offer a translation of this literature.

A paper recently published in Berlin, containing a *fac simile* of the hieroglyphic designs on pottery in the Berlin Museum, was then exhibited. They were in the pottery of Guatemala, with the same kind of picture-writing as was shown in the book. Nowhere else in America was pottery made with hieroglyphic writing, and, in Dr. Brinton's opinion, these painted vases were the work of men who pictured upon them the records of their tribe. The pottery was in this respect unlike that of North America, which was made by women. The designs on the vases were like those on the specimens recently acquired by the Museum of the University of Pennsylvania.

A series of very curious pictures made by the late Dr. Hermann Carl Berendt was then exhibited, illustrating the worship of the creative principle among the people of Central America. Dr. Berendt spent seventeen years in Mexico and Central America, collecting archæological material, and then met the fate of so many explorers, dying of a fever. The worship of creation as a distinct act was very widely extended over America. A study of the conventional representations, such as were exhibited, is very necessary. They were strictly priestly, and referred entirely to religious conceptions. By means of them the significance of one of the remarkable statuettes in the newly acquired collection in the University Museum became apparent.

Mr. Culin presented a brief *résumé* of a systematatic examination he recently made of the sports and games of children in
Corea. The Chinese influence was apparent in what might be
regarded as literary games, and he said that an analogue of the
familiar spelling puzzle, or word-building game, of New England
was played by Corean children at school.. The mystic concepts
in which certain games found their origin were much more apparent than in any of the children's games of Europe; and many of
the childish sports had a serious divinatory or expiatory association. The tug-of-war was played by people of villages and
districts to ascertain which would be the luckiest. Kites were
used as scapegoats, and at certain times would be released, with
an inscription that they were carrying away misfortune. Toys
were not numerous. They nearly all illustrated popular stories.
He said there were distinctive elements in Corean games, seemingly of an ethnical character, which promise to lead to conclusions of some importance.*

Mr. Harry Rogers exhibited some interesting coins, comprising two pattern fifty-dollar gold pieces and interesting crowns
of the sixteenth and seventeenth centuries.

OCTOBER 4TH, 1894.

Mr. Culin exhibited three large photographs of a group of
figures of Powhatan Indians, recently set up by Mr. Frank Hamilton Cushing on the Piney Branch of Rock Creek, just outside
the northwest boundary of the city of Washington; and read
a letter from Mr. Cushing, with the following particulars:

"The Powhatan Indian quarry figures, first exhibited at
Chicago, were modeled somewhat according to the 'Whyte pictures of the Virginia Indians. Guided by these, they were
dressed partly in prehistoric costumes, etc., found in a salt cave,
and partly in cinctures and ornaments made by me after the
Whyte pictures. Guided by these, also, I reconstructed a wigwam on the very site, as it turned out, where a similar one had
stood four or five centuries ago, close to an extensive chipping
ground, or workshop, on the borders of the knife-boulder quarries.
In one of the excavated quarries, two of the three figures are
represented working, while a third is roughly shaping knives

---

* Published in *Korean Games*, Philadelphia, 1896.

from the pebbles or spalls the others are throwing out. After I had built the little wigwam of a framework of saplings, arranged like the hoops of a hoop-wagon, and covered with rush and bark matting, I came to dig a place for the restoration hearth, which you see surmounted by a barbecue in front of the doorway of the hut. On digging I had the extraordinary experience to strike within six inches of the centre of an ancient stone-lined hearth! So, not only was the erection of a portable wigwam on the site of the old quarry and workshop proper as an addition to the scene, but it was actually, and I may say instinctively, placed by me on the very site of an ancient wigwam of about the same size. After the whole, hut and hearth, had been set up merely by topographic and likely indications, our digging revealed abundant evidences of camping: baking and boiling stones, used axes and hammers, sinkers, knives, and kitchen refuse. The scene may, then, be taken as accurately representing the Powhatan and Pamunkey Indians as they used to work here in the District of Columbia when quarrying the quartzite boulders of which were made their own knives, and the knives of the Indians they traded with in Maryland, Virginia, and the adjacent regions."

Mr. Culin exhibited specimens of American pottery from the Museum of the University of Pennsylvania. One, a vase from the Cramp collection of Guatemala pottery, consisted of a representation in pottery of a mace-gourd, over the upper part of which an engraved skin had been fastened with thongs, which bound it around the segments of the bowl. This vase, of exquisite shape, color, and design, illustrates the application of leather to gourd vessels in early times in Central America. The custom still survives in Mexico, as was well shown by a modern leather-covered flask, likewise exhibited, of native workmanship, purchased in Mexico by Dr. Robert H. Lamborn, and deposited by him in the University Museum.

A pottery vase made by the Mound Builders was then shown, which represented a gourd bowl bound in the same way with leather bands. Mr. Cushing has pointed out the value of the Mound pottery, of which the University possesses one of the largest collections in the world. By means of it the so-called Mound Builders, formerly regarded by many as a peculiar and mysterious people and a different race from the Indians of our day, are shown to have been one with the surviving stocks. He

PLATE VIII.

Market Street Bridge Monument.

has also shown that the fauna revealed by the pottery indicate that they were once a forest-dwelling people. Many of the vessels in the University's collection are simply copies in pottery of wooden trenchers that are still in use in the Northwest.

Mr. Culin also exhibited two pots that represented gourds completely covered with leather, even the original stitches being reproduced. A pottery bowl was also shown that retained an ancient leather band, put around it ages ago to bind it securely. It is clear from this pottery that much that has been regarded as decorative in American pottery is a survival from designs in other materials. Its forms are certainly copied from natural objects, and not the result of caprice, nor an attempt at ornament. The gradual conventionalizing of the types can be traced in the University's collection, which plainly tells the story of the unconscious origin of decorative ideas in America. They appear to have resulted from the interaction of the mythic conceptions and the practical demands of everyday life.

Mr. Westcott Bailey spoke of the condition of the old monument at the corner of Twenty-third and Market Streets, which was erected about 1804. He thought that, if the attention of the authorities was called to it, steps would be taken for its preservation. He believed the monument formerly stood in the centre of the street near the rise of the bridge. It was voted that a committee be appointed to view the monument and report to the Society. The President appointed Messrs. Westcott Bailey, R. H. Lamborn, and Harry Rogers.

It was voted that Mr. Culin be reimbursed the cost of a complete collection of U. S. postal currency bought for exhibition in the Society's collection at Madrid.

It was voted that the Society's collection of paper money be deposited in Memorial Hall, and that Mr. Dorr be consulted in the matter.

NOVEMBER 4TH, 1894.

The death was announced of Mr. Samuel M. Smedley, Resident Member, July 21st, 1894; and of Col. Garrick Mallery, Corresponding Member, October 24th, 1894.

Mr. Julius Kumpei Matsumoto, a visitor, read by invitation a paper on the "Origin of the Japanese Race." *

---

* Afterwards published in the *Japan Mail*, Yokohama.

The President. Dr. D. G. Brinton, strongly opposed the theory advanced by Mr. Matsumoto that the so-called Yamato race of Japan were descended from the Hittites; and urged that we do not know anything about the language, culture or history of the Hittites, in spite of what Prof. Sayce has said. Prof. Heinrich Winkler seems to have clearly shown that the Yamato race is Siberic or Turanian.

Mr. Lyman said he agreed with Mr. Matsumoto that there were probably three races in Japan: the Ainos, a Malayan race, and what Mr. Matsumoto called the Yamato race, which last had apparently come to Japan by way of Corea. As the stay in Corea was doubtless somewhat prolonged, it may be said that as Coreans they invaded Japan. That seems far enough to go back at present; and it is quite natural that invaders should have come from Corea, since there is an island between the two countries from which both may be seen. The opinion is corroborated by the strong likeness said to exist between the Corean and Japanese languages. It seems fanciful at present to argue that the Coreans came from any special race that inhabited Western Asia in very ancient times. It has been maintained that the Ainos first inhabited Japan, even in the southwest; that Coreans came from the west; and that a Malay race came from the south and conquered those already on the islands. Jimmu Tenno, called the first human emperor, from whom the present dynasty claims to have originated, is first mentioned as in the extreme southwest.

The following paper by Mr. Clarence B. Moore, on "The Boro Budur Temple of Java," was read, in his absence, by Mr. Inman Horner:

Boro Budur Temple.

THE BORO BUDUR TEMPLE OF JAVA.

BY CLARENCE B. MOORE.

It could doubtless be asserted with perfect truth that to the great majority of cultivated persons—persons to whom the Acropolis, the Colosseum, and the Pyramids are almost household words,—the name even of the wonderful lava temple in the heart of Java, the Boro Budur, is entirely unknown. Yet, perhaps, in certain respects the Boro Bodur fully equals any now-existing monument of bygone ages; and it is difficult to explain the general lack of information concerning it, except that travelers to Java rarely get beyond Batavia, or possibly Buitenzorg, and then hasten away to Singapore to continue the beaten track of the "globe-trotter." Moreover, it is almost as hard to obtain information of these ruins in Batavia as it would be in New York.

Batavia is an interesting town, mainly in that one can there best see the very free and easy customs and costumes of the East Indian Dutch. All over the houses and hotels, until time to prepare for dinner, at four or five P. M., the women go about clad in camisoles of linen, with the sarong, or short skirt, reaching half way to the ankle, with stockingless feet thrust into slippers and hair hanging loosely down the back. The sarongs are of the most gaudy colors, and the wearers seem to vie with each other in selecting patterns striking and bizarre to the last degree, in which snakes, dragons, and devils play a prominent part. The retail trade of Java is monopolized by the Chinese, and the hotel is haunted by these people, pack in hand.

From Batavia to Samarang is a two-days' sail, and fortunate it is that the weather is usually calm, for those having a tendency towards seasickness and a consequent horror of tobacco smoke *pro tem.* would otherwise have a hard time. From morning to night, on deck, in the cabin and staterooms, the smoking goes on, a tumbler upside down serving as a rest for the cigar, while the smoker between puffs snatches time to masticate his food. On deck a long piece of lighted punk lies upon a stand in the form of a gilded dragon, and, like the sacred flame of Vesta, is never permitted to die out; a native stands by, ever ready to answer the demand for *api* (fire, in Malay), and to carry the punk

83

to any one wishing a light. At Samarang there was almost no one able to give information as to the itinerary to pursue, but it was explained that an interpreter would be absolutely necessary, inasmuch as nobody in the interior could speak anything save Dutch or Malay. After a long search, the services of a lad of about seventeen, the son of a German tailor, were secured.

Less than three hours by rail from Samarang is the town of Solo, with a much better hotel than one might expect under the circumstances. About two hours more by rail bring the traveler to Brambanan, which place, next to the Boro Budur, contains the most interesting ruins in Java.

The ruins at Brambanan cover a comparatively large area and are mainly interesting for what they must have been, since great havoc has been wrought by the roots of trees, which, extending in all directions, have torn apart the masses of masonry. The stones composing the walls of the various temples are grooved, and fit each other, no cement being used. A number of statues are scattered around, which the traveler from India readily recognizes as representing various gods belonging to the Brahminical pantheon.

In the ruins of Chandi Sewu, or the Thousand Temples, which form part of the remains at Brambanan, are a number of figures apparently of Buddha; though it has been asserted that such is not the case, and that these effigies of stone represent simply votaries in the act of devotion to the Brahminical gods of the place. These figures are the same as all those found at the temple of Boro Budur, and have all the attributes seen in effigies of Buddha elsewhere.

From Brambanan to Djokjokarta is a journey of only half an hour, also by rail. The town of Djokjokarta is the capital of a native Sultan, and has an interesting "water palace" and a large collection of leopards all huddled together into an enormous wooden cage. These beasts are the property and the pride of the Sultan, and are entirely untamed, to all appearance, as they do not hesitate to spring at any outsider whose curiosity draws him into too close proximity to the bars of their wooden home.

If desired, the journey to the Boro Budur can be made in a coach-and-four, the distance being twenty-five miles over a fine broad road, as smooth as a floor and lined with native villages, shaded by towering cocoanut and palm. If a market day, the villagers can be seen, either squatting by the road-

PLATE X.

side offering for sale small heaps of food or merchandise, or moving from trader to trader making purchases here and there as their fancy prompts.

It is a journey never to be forgotten, and the drive is all too soon over, when at length the temple of Boro Budur looms in sight. The traveler having previously, in all probability, met no one who has ever seen this wonderful structure, and having heard but the vaguest hints as to its size, and nothing relating to its wealth of statues and bas-reliefs, is fairly dazed. Upon him who has previously seen the temples of Egypt, of Greece, and of India, Baalbec, in Syria, and the wonderful ruins of Girgenti, if ruins they may be called, where the ravages of time are scarcely apparent, and the altar and stairways stand intact—who has lingered among the baths, aqueducts and amphitheatres of Italy and the South of France—it is doubtful if the first impressions of these wonders of architecture in any way equal the effect produced by this lava temple in the heart of Java. When one has seen pictures of famous ruins and photographs in great numbers, and for years read and heard descriptions of the most enthusiastic kind, it is seldom that the reality very far surpasses the preconceived idea. The effect of the Boro Budur is almost stunning, so unexpected is the grandeur of the sight presented.

On the top of an eminence, which has been leveled to some extent to receive it, is the temple of Boro Budur. It is not quite square, but nearly so, each side being about 620 feet in length; it is entirely built of blocks of black lava, excessively hard, to which quality, doubtless, it owes its excellent state of preservation.

It consists of seven ranges of walls and terraces decreasing in size until they culminate in a level space, in the centre of which stands a species of dome about fifty feet in diameter, containing a gigantic statue of Buddha. This dome is surrounded by three circles of towers constructed of lattice-work of stone, each enshrining an image of Buddha, seventy-two in all. Descending, one passes to successive terraces, the walls of which on the inside are covered with bas-reliefs illustrating everything pertaining to the life of the forgotten race which flourished when the temple was built. These bas-reliefs are executed in a high style of art, and are, all together, over two miles in length. On the outside of the terraces, at regular intervals, are sitting images of Buddha, which certainly number not less than four hundred and

PLATE XII.

Lion at foot of Boro Budur stairway.

beyond the rank vegetation and an occasional earthquake. The inhabitants of Java are now Mohammedan and have no traditions relating to the temples of their island, though they still regard the images with a certain reverence. When we consider the mighty mass of masonry, the extreme hardness of the lava, and the great extent and endless variety of the bas-reliefs, it becomes a question whether any architectural remains now existing can compare, in the amount of labor expended, with these wonderful ruins in the interior of Java.

The great Buddhist temples of Ankor, in Cambodia, are so difficult of access and so far removed from the beaten track, that a failure to visit them may readily find excuse; but for the antiquary or the traveler of cultivation reaching Singapore, it is surely a mistake of magnitude to omit a journey to the lava temple of Boro Budur.

Dr. Robert H. Lamborn exhibited specimens of the ordinary tableware of the ancient Romans, commonly known as Samian ware, and found wherever the Roman legions penetrated. One of the pieces, from the Lamborn collection in the University Museum, was found by Mr. Waldo Story at Arezzo. This ware was first formed on the wheel. One specimen bore the stamp of the maker, together with a scratched inscription, probably the name of the original owner.

A discussion ensued upon the presence of glazed ware in American pottery. Its existence has been denied by many authorities; but Dr. Lamborn considered the question practically settled by specimens in the Cramp collection in the University Museum.

President Brinton described the method of finishing pottery among the ancient Mexicans. There are two processes, one being the application of a slip of clay to the ware after its first baking. If the clay contained saline matter it would, on re-baking, give the appearance of a glaze; but he did not regard such glazing as intentional.

Dr. Lamborn said that what he considered to be glaze on the Cramp pottery was doubtless produced in that way.

Dr. Lamborn exhibited a large green stone ear-ring from Mexico, and a jewel of rock crystal from the Sioux of North Dakota, the latter set in leather bound with beads. He regarded this jewel as a remarkable illustration of the first steps towards the use of stones in personal ornament.

Mr. Westcott Bailey reported for the committee on the monument at Twenty-third and Market Streets; and it was voted that the report be offered for publication in some daily newspaper.

A committee, with Mr. Franklin Platt as chairman, was appointed to nominate officers and standing committees for next year.

DECEMBER 6TH, 1894.

The death was announced of Hon. Robert C. Winthrop, Honorary Vice-President of this Society for Massachusetts, November 16th, 1894.

The President, Dr. D. G. Brinton, gave a *résumé* of a paper it had been announced he would read on some objects in the Poinsett collection in the Academy of Natural Sciences; but the paper was not yet completed.

Mr. Carl Edelheim exhibited a number of antique rings, including an Egyptian scarab in its original setting, a white gold ring, and others.

Mr. Edelheim also presented to the Society four specimens of Roman coins, for which special thanks were voted.

Mr. Culin exhibited a painted vase from the great pyramid of Cholula, in Mexico.

President Brinton said the vase was inscribed repeatedly with the first of the characters of the Mexican Book of Days. The great pyramid of Cholula was the religious centre of Anahuac at the time of the Conquest, and was unquestionably the largest artificial structure in the world.

Mr. Westcott Bailey, of the committee on the Market Street bridge monument made an additional report; and expressed the committee's disappointment that the publication of their former report had not induced the descendants of those mentioned on the monument to come forward and aid in its restoration.

Mr. Culin read a recommendation from Mr. Geo. F. Kunz requesting him to coöperate in an effort to secure better designs for the coinage of the United States. The matter was referred to the Committee on Numismatics.

It was voted that Mr. Culin be authorized to remove the library of the Society to the University of Pennsylvania, the books to remain in his personal charge and be accessible to members of the Society.

On motion of Mr. Cornelius Stevenson, it was voted that the Society's real estate at the southeast corner of Twenty-first and Pine Streets be sold to Messrs. Hoben & Doyle for $6,500.

Mr. Franklin Platt, chairman of the committee on nominations, reported that the committee had renominated the entire body of officers and standing committees, with the addition of Prof. F. W. Putnam, of Cambridge, Mass., in the place of the lately deceased Hon. Robert C. Winthrop, as Honorary Vice-President for Massachusetts. The nominations were by vote declared closed, and the whole list of officers and committees was unanimously elected.

JANUARY 3D.

Mr. Francis Jordan, Jr., read a paper, in which he accounted for the mound known as the "the Hummock," in Great Bay, at Tuckerton, near Atlantic City, New Jersey, by the theory that it was originally a pile dwelling.

Thereupon a discussion ensued, in which the opinion was expressed that the present rate of subsidence of the Atlantic coast of the United States was quite enough to account for the existence of the submerged land around the hummock; and it was doubted that this was originally a pile dwelling. Many instances of the effect of subsidence were adduced by Mr. Iüngerich, Mr. Platt, and others. Mr. Platt was invited by the President to prepare a paper on the influence of geological subsidence or elevation upon the antiquities of the Atlantic coast.

Mr. Cornelius Stevenson exhibited a sword hilt that had belonged to Prince Eugene of Savoy, from the collection of Prince Lichtenstein, of Vienna. A passport of Prince Eugene accompanied the sword, and was also exhibited. Mr. Stevenson read a written description of the ornamentation of the hilt and of its significance, with an account of its history. The object excited lively interest, and was discussed by President Brinton and others.

Mr. Carl Edelheim exhibited a ring with the arms of Ostend; and two rings with the signs of the zodiac, one silver and one gold.

Mr. Culin said these two rings were made by negroes of the west coast of Africa, similar rings having been made in the so-called Dahomey village at the Columbian. Exposition.

Mr. Culin exhibited an early English silver penny and three Irish silver pennies, one of William and Mary, and one of Elizabeth. He also exhibited specimens of early Roman coinage.

FEBRUARY 7TH, 1895.

The death was announced of Dr. Robert H. Lamborn, Resident Member and Vice-President of the Society, on the 14th of January.

The President, Dr. D. G. Brinton, spoke *extempore* on the life of Dr. Lamborn and his services to science. They had both been born in the same county and within a year of each other; but first met in Paris in 1860, when both were students—Dr. Lamborn, of mining, and Dr. Brinton, of medicine. Dr. Lamborn published some metallurgical works in early life, at the time of his studies in Germany and France. He never lost sight of the higher elements of culture, and in later life made large collections, which he rendered freely accessible to all students. One of the last acts of his life was to offer a prize for the best essay on what constitutes the highest type of an American citizen. Dr. Brinton had been one of the judges to award the prize; and, in his opinion, Dr. Lamborn himself closely typified the ideal as expressed in the two essays to which the prize was given.

Mr. Franklin Platt spoke briefly on the submergence of the sea-coast, in compliance with the request made at the last meeting. The surface of the earth, he said, is in a state of movement, there being no stability to the crust of the earth. There is a great motion, from the centre of the continent down to the coast line, which is not to be attributed to the shrinking of the crust of the earth. The coast of Texas is sinking. Florida has sunk one thousand feet. From North Carolina northeastward we have submerged forests of our own modern period, and probably since the glacial period. Prof. McGee says that our coast has sunk two feet in a century; others say one foot. We have practically no means of historical comparison, as, for instance, Holland has. Holland has sunk at the rate of four inches in a century since 1732, and at an average rate of one foot in a century during the last one thousand years. It has gone down some twenty-five to thirty feet, and cost Holland more than sixty million dollars. In Sweden, the southern end is sinking and the northern rising. The coast of China is sinking. The islands off the coast have the same fauna as the mainland; and there is no evidence that the islands have long been separated from the coast. It is supposed that Africa is sinking less than any other continental area. Australia has changed very little. The sinking has been continuous, uninterrupted by periods of elevation. In all cases, wherever we find prehistoric human relics at tidewater, the probable subsidence should not be overlooked.

Mr Lyman called attention to the fact that according to Prof. Salisbury there have been repeated depressions and elevations on the New Jersey coast. He cited three periods of elevation, two of them since the beginning of the glacial epoch, all preceded by depression. The last elevation was forty to sixty feet or more; and was followed by the present subsidence. (See R. D. Salisbury, New Jersey State Geological Report for 1892, pp. 164-166.)

President Brinton spoke of the shell heaps as among the important objects we have to study along the Atlantic coast. They occur from the coast of Florida northward to Maine, and probably further. The remains appear to be of considerable antiquity. Some have been completely washed away, either by simple erosion or by subsidence. He said the submergence seemed to have been in a series of curves, and that with the depression there was also local warping upward.

Mr. Culin exhibited several specimens of American aboriginal pottery of remarkable beauty and finish, recently acquired by the Archæological Museum of the University. One consisted of a cylinder of pottery about two and a half inches in length, with a longitudinal perforation. The cylinder had probably been used for applying pigment; and on the face was a design twice repeated of conventional animal forms. The cylinder was intended to produce a continuous pattern. Another specimen, a small vase, had the form of a very symmetrical human head, bearing twelve circles in a continuous line, one within the other on each cheek. They probably indicated paint or tatooing. Another vase bore the head of an owl; another, a human face. A fragment with an animal's head was also shown. The exact place of manufacture was not known; but the objects were believed to be of South American type, and probably from Ecuador.

It was voted that the next meeting of the Society be held at the Penn Club, and that each member have the privilege of inviting a guest.

MARCH 7TH, 1895.

The Society met at the Penn Club House, and as invitations had been issued for a reception, twenty guests were present besides twenty members.

David Milne was requested to act as Recording Secretary, in the absence of Mr. Culin.

President Brinton spoke briefly of the objects of the Society. It was founded in 1858 as a Numismatic Society, but, later on, the study of archæology was included within its province. In this latter field it is more liberal in its scope than many kindred societies, and is in no wise sectional in its investigations. Yet it examines local antiquities, and has taken measures for their protection and preservation.

The significance of the present can be understood only by a knowledge of the past, the indices of the past being essential to a comprehension of man's tendencies and development and of all that pertains to his history. Within the present generation, archæology has made enormous strides, especially in directing men's thoughts to philosophical and spiritual matters as distinguished from material things. It promotes culture and better aims, leading men to a higher excellence in modes and standards of thought, elevating them to a plane where they seek for the perfection of the ideal.

Mr. Chas. E. Dana exhibited a papal medal of the year 1653; also an Arabian compass, such as the Mohammedans use to ascertain the direction of Mecca, before they pray, when traveling.

Mr. Harry Rogers showed a large number of bronze French medals of the Napoleonic period, the majority of them being commemorative of events in the life of the Emperor. As almost every event from the rise until the fall of the power of Napoleon the First was so commemorated, the result was a series of medals unequalled for completeness. The types were executed with great care and skill, the designs being in the classic style which distinguished the French art of that time.

Mr. J. Colvin Randall showed a powder horn of the American Revolution, which he had obtained in Birmingham. One side was covered with a patriotic inscription.*

Mr. J. S. Patterson called the attention of the Society to reputed aboriginal traces in the limestone cave near Port Kennedy, Montgomery County, Pa. The President said the Academy of Natural Sciences was examining the find.

Two silver coins shown by a guest were identified as Spanish-American.

---

*See *Bulletin, Free Museum of Science and Art*, University of Pennsylvania, Vol. I, No. 3.

Mr. F. M. Day, a guest, gave an outline of a lecture on the Pantheon, which had lately been delivered by Prof. Ware at the University of Pennsylvania.

President Brinton called attention to a theory advanced by a resident of Savannah, that Florida had been occupied at an early age by a people highly civilized. Many land and water marks had been selected for triangulation in making a complete survey of the land and harbors, which this gentleman is able to designate. President Brinton considered that this theory has some corroboration in external evidence which he is now investigating.

Capt. Collum said he would submit to the Society for its inspection and opinion a bronze head which he thought had come from India.

APRIL 4TH, 1895.

The death of Dr. W. S. W. Ruschenberger, Vice-President of the Society, was announced, March 24th, 1895 in his 88th year.

Mr. Cornelius Stevenson exhibited some specimens of historic arms that he had recently acquired from Germany, and that were formerly in the Royal Armory at Dresden. One, a wheel-lock gun, once belonged to the Elector of Saxony, and bore his arms and the date 1560. With it, as an appurtenance, there was a velvet-covered baldric. Small, tubular boxes of tin were hung from the baldric, and had been used to contain the individual charges of powder. Mr. Stevenson also exhibited a morion, inlaid with gold, that belonged to the same Elector.

The President, Dr. D. G. Brinton, gave a brief account of the recent explorations in the caves of Europe, Asia, and America. He said they yielded results entirely at variance with generally accepted theories. French and German archæologists in Europe, and Mr. Henry C. Mercer in America, have made explorations that have revolutionized our ideas about primitive man. The caves in Asia Minor, Syria, and Palestine, and the caves first explored by Mr. Mercer in America, yielded no traces of man associated with extinct animals, as the caves of France and Germany had done. And now Mr. Mercer returns from Yucatan with the same story from that country. He has found nothing there that carries us back to a period more remote than the time of the existing Indians. He finds only man later than the latest extinct animals. The story has already been reversed that man originated somewhere in Eastern Asia. The caves of that region, where his remains, if he existed there, should naturally be found do not yield a trace of early man, such as has been discovered in Europe. The absence of remains of earliest man in those regions points to his having originated in some quarter, just where we do not know, where he developed up to a certain degree of culture.

Mr. Culin made a brief communication with reference to the recent acquisitions of the University Museum.

Mr. John W. Townsend exhibited a Chinese fan of the last century, made of metal inlaid with enamel. The form was that of European fans of the First Empire.

Mr. Westcott Bailey exhibited a two-sous piece struck at Strasburg in the fifth year of Liberty, 1793; and a Washington penny, with the head of Washington crowned with a laurel wreath.

The Corresponding Secretary exhibited a handsome book, *Numismata Londinensia*, lately presented to the Society by the Library Committee of the City of London. It contains an account, with beautiful illustrations, of the medals struck by that city in commemoration of important municipal events, 1831-1893. Special thanks were voted.

Mr. Westcott Bailey reported for the committee on the Market Street bridge monument that he had placed the papers in the hands of Mr. Audenried, who had promised to bring the matter to the attention of the City Council.

MAY 2D, 1895.

Mr. Henry C. Mercer gave an account of the caves of Yucatan lately visited by him. The mountains of Yucatan are honeycombed with caves. The direct object of his search was the vestiges of early man in those caves. Unlike other caves he had explored, they are entered, like wells, from an opening in the top, through which one must let himself down with ropes, by the roots of trees, or by the rude ladders built by the Indians. At first it appeared unlikely that such caves would furnish the evidence desired, on account of their difficulty of access; but he soon discovered that they were the only places where water could be obtained in the dry season, and that they must have been resorted to by any people living in that country. There is no surface water, running springs, or brooks in Yucatan. This fact led the Indians of the earliest times to enter the caves. All of the caves contained human remains, and large stone dishes to catch the water that trickles down from the roof; and the floor is covered with fragments of pottery.

The caves are illuminated by circular openings where the thin crust has broken through at the top. Trees have thrown down their roots through this orifice, vegetation has sprung up luxuriantly, all presenting a fairy-like scene in the light diffused from the opening above. The caves vary greatly in their character, some being intensely hot, others cool; some are comparatively easy of access, others difficult; some drip water from the stalactites, while others are now dry; and some are dens of wild beasts and are dreaded by the Indians. The walls of some of the caves bear petroglyphs, not hieroglyphs in the true sense, but pictures and incised lines. In one cave a projecting stalagmite was cut into the form of an ape's head. It was the cave floor, however, that was the object of the explorer's attack. Trenches were dug in the floor down to the bed-rock. Sections of the cave floors were illustrated by diagrams, and shown to consist of cave earth with bands of ashes and mold, filled with fragments of pottery. The pottery did not vary from top to bottom, and that in the lower layers was polished like that at the top. There were no traces of any other people, of paleolithic man, or of any Indians other than the Mayas, whose descendants still resort to the caves.

Lotan was one of the most interesting and beautiful of the caves. It was entered by a steep incline, followed by stone steps and ladders made of saplings, the work of the Indians. Passing through a narrow passage, within which there were stone walls, apparently barriers against intrusion, one entered a great chamber, 350 feet in height, with a natural skylight at the top. Openings in the great chamber led into passages in which the explorer might easily lose his way.

As the result of his work, Mr. Mercer concluded that the people on first coming to the cave possessed the art of making pottery; and, therefore, that the Mayas developed their culture elsewhere before they came to Yucatan. As nothing was found below their remains, there was no paleolithic man, and no other Indian than the Maya, in Yucatan. Compared with some cave deposits of Europe, they are much more recent. There did not appear to be any remains of pleistocene animals, though the few

7

bones found have not been critically examined. Only three or four arrow-heads were found. From that fact Mr. Mercer concluded they were not hunters, and also that they had no domestic animals. He re-examined his conclusion that the floor reached represented the real bottom; but the affirmative evidence seemed decisive.*

The President, Dr. D. G. Brinton, said that these important and novel observations corresponded with the traditions of the Mayas, who, according to their accounts, first appeared in the country in the second or third century of our era. Their records seem to imply that they found it uninhabited.

President Brinton spoke of the excavations made by Mr. Gerard Fowke along the Charles River, near Cambridge, Mass., and of his discovery of supposed work of the Northmen. He also spoke of the two Runic inscriptions that had recently been found on the Atlantic coast of America, one near Cambridge, Mass., and one on the line between New York City and Westchester County. He said he had examined both inscriptions with great care; and was satisfied that they were in Runic characters. The only question was whether they were modern frauds or authentic.

A discussion ensued on the question of Runic inscriptions in America, particularly the Yarmouth inscription, referred to by Mr. Culin. President Brinton expressed a favorable opinion as to its genuineness and to the probability that remains of the Pre-Columbian Norse settlers had been found in Eastern America.

Mr. Harry Rogers exhibited a number of medals figured in the work *Numismata Londinensia*, presented at the last meeting, comprising: "In honor of Her Majesty's visit to the Corporation of London, November 9th, 1837"; Alexander II, of Russia; Napoleon III and Eugénie; New Coal Exchange opened, November 30th, 1849; Alexandra, March, 1863.

Mr. Henry Jüngerich presented to the Society a number of specimens of Continental money, and copies of early American newspapers.

On motion of Mr. F. D. Langenheim, Curator of Numismatics, it was voted that the Committee on Numismatics be authorized to dispose of any or all duplicates in the Society's

---

* See *Hill Caves of Yucatan*. By Henry C. Mercer. Philadelphia, 1896.

collection now deposited in Memorial Hall, and to purchase with the proceeds any pieces needed to complete the series of United States coins.

Mr. Cornelius Stevenson, of the committee on the sale of the property at Twenty-first and Pine Streets, reported that the sale had been completed; and at his request the committee was discharged.

The Treasurer, Mr. Harry Rogers, made a report, showing a balance on hand of $710.57. Mr. Franklin Platt and Mr. Charles D. Clark were appointed a committee to audit the Treasurer's accounts.

OCTOBER 3D, 1895.

Mr. Carl Edelheim exhibited the contents of a burial urn from Hungary, consisting of bronze ornaments and glass and amber beads. One of the objects was a bracelet terminating at one end in a hand and at the other in a phallus. Mr. Cushing spoke of the significance of the same combination of symbols in America, where among the Pueblos a similar ornament is worn by women who have borne children.

Prof. Maxwell Sommerville exhibited an interesting Hindoo ring.

The Curator of Numismatics, Mr. F. D. Langenheim, reported that the catalogue of the Society's coins in Memorial Hall had been completed, comprising 4,119 coins and 281 pieces of paper money. A copy of the catalogue was exhibited by the Curator. He read a letter from Mr. Dalton Dorr, requesting the Society to appoint a day for a private view of its collections.

NOVEMBER 7TH, 1895.

Vice-President Maxwell Sommerville exhibited a series of photographs of Chinese laborers, obtained from a factor at Singapore. Various types were represented. Each man was photographed with his name written in Chinese characters on a slip of paper pinned on his blouse. Copies of the printed contracts between the employers and laborers were also shown, one in Chinese and another in English. The term of service is for three years. An advance of thirty dollars is made by the em-

ployer. Prof. Sommerville also related a number of interesting
incidents of his recent travels in Eastern Asia.

The Curator of Numismatics, Mr. F. D. Langenheim, reported
that he had secured a proof set of the United States coins of
1895; and that in the Society's coin collection there were 921
duplicates, many of no numismatic value. Also, that Mr. J.
Sergeant Price kindly gives the Society permission to use the dies
from which the medal presented to the Society by his late father
was struck. There is no copy of the Price medal in the collection
of the Society at Memorial Hall. The Curator requested that the
Society fix a day to visit the collection at Memorial Hall and
make the formal transfer. The matter was referred to the officers of the Society with power to act.

Messrs. Franklin Platt, Cornelius Stevenson, and Westcott
Bailey were appointed a committee to nominate candidates for
officers and standing committees for the annual election at the
next meeting.

DECEMBER 5TH, 1895.

The President, Dr. D. G. Brinton, spoke of Mayan pottery,
and said it may be considered to be the most perfect work of
any primitive American potters. A comparative study of Central American pottery reveals the essential identity of the pottery of Coban, in Guatemala, with that of Copan, in Honduras,
and that of Palenque, in Tobasco; an identity that extends
through all the pottery of the region from Honduras on the
east to Tobasco and Chiapas on the west. This pottery is
clearly different from the Mayan pottery of Yucatan. The
Mayas did not begin their history in Yucatan. Mr. Mercer's
observations show conclusively that they were the first people
to enter the country. Their pottery supplies proofs of their independent development in the peninsula, and bears out the Maya
tradition ; and equally accords with Mr. Mercer's observations.
In illustration, President Brinton exhibited a number of pictures
and some unpublished photographs of Mayan pottery in several
European museums, as well as two jars from the Archæological
Museum of the University of Pennsylvania. One, a painted vase
from Huehuetenango, he said, was the finest specimen of American pottery in existence, a conclusion he had arrived at after
a careful study of the collections of the Museums of the Troca-

déro at Paris, the British Museum, the Leyden Museum, and the Peabody Museum at Cambridge. The other vase bears incised ornaments, and ranks as the most important known specimen of its kind.

Prof. Maxwell Sommerville exhibited a series of heart-shaped ornaments worn by women in Southern India, with photographs of native women wearing the ornament both as costume and decoration. The specimens were of various materials: base metal set with plates of colored glass, and one of gold with designs in high relief.

Mr Carl Edelheim exhibited some interesting personal ornaments, including a marble cameo from Pompeii, and two silver gilt peasant-rings from Altenburg.

He spoke also of the bust of the Emperor Hadrian in the University Museum.

Mr. Westcott Bailey exhibited a fresh-water pearl of great beauty and extremely curious from Wisconsin.

Mr. Henry Iüngerich exhibited a Roman lamp obtained from the excavations conducted by the Emperor Napoleon in Rome in 1860; and a curious modern lamp with religious emblems, the precise use of which has not been definitely ascertained.

Mr. Culin spoke of the Corean alphabet, suggesting a probable origin for it in 'the counting sticks used in Eastern Asia for arithmetical operations. The alphabet seems to be a direct invention and of remarkable simplicity.

The Curator of Numismatics, Mr. F. D. Langenheim, laid the catalogue of its coins before the Society.

It was voted to accept Mr. Dalton Dorr's invitation to visit the coin collection at Memorial Hall at 3 P. M., Saturday, December 14th.

The nominating committee reported a list of candidates for officers and standing committees for the coming year. The whole list were elected, as well as the still-living Honorary Vice-Presidents of 1895. (See page 9.)

JANUARY 2D.

The President, Dr. D. G. Brinton, delivered his annual address, taking for his subject, "The Results of Recent Digging," and referring to the most important excavations that have been made during the past year in various parts of the world. In Egypt, Mr. Flinders-Petrie, from January to March, discovered a new race, which he considers to belong to the time from about the seventh to the tenth dynasties. This people introduced an entirely new civilization into the Nile Valley, equal in many respects to what they found there; a people less developed in some ways and higher in others than the Egyptians. They excelled in stone working, as shown in their sickles, chipped and polished down to a fine edge, almost like those we are accustomed to see of iron. They did not, however, have the architecture or the architectural tendencies of the Egyptians. They appear to have finally died out, or been absorbed. Mr. Petrie has suggested that they came from the land of the west, and has identified them with the Berbers, the Numidians, and Libyans of ancient times.

Dr. Brinton then spoke of the latest explorations at Troy. Dr. Schliemann did not live to complete his investigations. Through the generosity of his widow and of certain German scholars, excavations have been continued through the past year by Dr. Dörpfield. They prove that Dr. Schliemann was mistaken in some of his conclusions regarding Troy. He regarded the second city as the Homeric one; but these later explorations show it was the fourth city that was the Troy of the epic, a city, indeed, much larger than Dr. Schliemann had any idea of. It may now be seen that Troy was contemporary with Argos, Mycenæ, and Tiryns, and was destroyed about the time that Homer and the others claim for it, and that it was destroyed by tribes sweeping down from the north, and that the Trojan war was but a mere episode in that migration.

Turning to Babylonia, Dr. Brinton said the investigations of the Department of Archæology of the University of Pennsylvania had made what may be regarded as the leading discovery of the past year in Assyria. He referred to the excavations at Niffer, an ancient city southeast of the site of the city of Babylon. A year or so ago, the cylinders seemed to indicate that the explorers had reached the site of the First Sargon, 3500 to 3700 B. C. They then came upon a solid pavement, upon which were placed the foundations of the temple of Sargon. Last year, on digging through that pavement, another city was found, in which the cylinders found carry back recorded history 500 to 700 years further; so that we can now trace Babylonian history to 4300 or 4500 B. C.

As to digging in the New World, the Mexican government made a series of investigations at Teotihuacan, at the suggestion of some Mexican antiquaries, and with a desire to provide something of special interest for the Congress of Americanists held at Mexico last autumn by the invitation of that government. The Teotihuacan ruins are regarded as the most extensive and most remarkable in America. There are two pyramids, one of the Sun and one of the Moon, as they are called. On digging alongside of one of them, it was found, instead of having its base close at hand, to extend far beneath the present surface of the ground. The sides exposed by the digging were found to be covered with stucco and painted with symbolic designs in brilliant colors. According to Prof. Frederick Starr, of Chicago, a great mass of earth appears to have been deposited around the pyramid by the hand of man. We have here another buried city, surpassing in extent the wildest fancy.

Again, at Chama, in northeastern Guatemala, a coffee-planter from Hamburg, named Dieseldorf, has been examining the many mounds of that district. Some of the results of his work were brought before the Society at the last meeting. He discovered remains of a people of the highest type, including a number of painted vases now in the Berlin Museum.

Finally, in Yucatan, the work carried on by Mr. Henry C. Mercer, at great personal sacrifices of time and health, have results of great importance in the line of history. He has clearly established that the Mayas brought their culture to the peninsula; but it is not yet certain that he found the culture layers of the earliest man that existed in Yucatan.

Mr. John T. Morris exhibited a beautiful funeral statuette of an Egyptian mummy, made of painted wood, with a receptacle at the back in which a papyrus hád been placed.

Mr. Culin argued that, from analogues in Chinese culture, where wooden idols have a similar receptacle at the back for Sanscrit or old Chinese sacred and magical writings, inserted in order to vitalize the images, we may conclude the use of the "papyrus case," so called, had originally a similar purpose.

Mr. Morris also gave an account of observations in Egypt during his recent visit. At Luxor, a small steam engine was seen. Some said it was to be used in pumping out the lake, for the recovery of treasures of great value believed to have been thrown into it by the ancient Egyptians. Others declared the pumping was to prevent the destruction of the ruins of Karnak by gradual undermining. The greatest effort is made to preserve the columns by digging trenches around them; but so far without success. The ruins of Egypt, he said, are generally in fine condition. At Thebes, the rubbish is getting removed. The excavations are protected from intrusion, and no photographs are allowed to be made. He also exhibited a beautiful funeral case of terra-cotta, with two cartouches; likewise, two very beautiful and perfect molds for the glazed green porcelain images, of which he showed a remarkable specimen.

Mr. Henry Iüngerich exhibited a miniature of Washington, that had an authentic history for at least sixty years.

Prof. Maxwell Sommerville exhibited two very large and perfect spear-heads of green bottle glass, made by the aborigines of northern Australia; also, an object of carved stone (Fig. 4) found

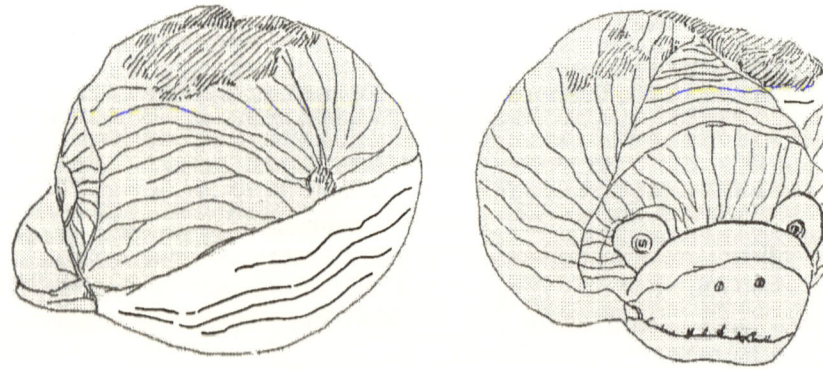

Fig. 4.

on the banks of the Delaware, on the New Jersey side, below Montague, the occasion of a lively discussion. It was a natural stone of rounded form, apparently a nodule of the carbonate of iron. It was carved with fine lines into the representation of an animal, perhaps a tortoise, or possibly a beaver, or otter. The head, with eyes, nostrils, and teeth, was clearly defined.

President Brinton congratulated the Society on the admirable arrangement of its coins now displayed at Memorial Hall. He said that on the 14th of December, 1895, the collection was opened with a formal ceremony, and that the President had made an address and the President of the Pennsylvania Museum had responded. The arrangement of the coins had been effected by the devoted labors of the Curator of Numismatics, Mr. F. D. Langenheim, of the Director of the Pennsylvania Museum, Mr. Dalton Dorr, and of Mr. H. M. Wilder, upon whom had devolved the work of identification and cataloguing.

Special thanks were voted to each of those three.

FEBRUARY 6TH, 1896.

The President, Dr. D. G. Brinton, spoke of prehistoric metal work. It is generally accepted that the earliest use of metals was not one invention or discovery. The first metal that appears to have attracted the attention of man was copper. That was especially true in the New World. The Indians of this vicinity obtained their copper from northern New Jersey. They did not, however, know how to smelt or fuse it; nor has a single implement of smelted metal been found among any tribe within the United States or northward. It is doubtful whether we can rightly speak of any of them as in the metal age. The art of smelting was known in Mexico, Central America, and Peru. It is probably an error to suppose that the art of smelting copper was introduced from Peru into those more northern countries. The use of the precious metals was also known in Mexico and Peru. There are few instances of the use of iron in America, either for ornament or for weapons.

The use of bronze began in Western Europe about 1500 B. C. It was known in Egypt 3000 to 4000 B. C. It was known in Eastern Africa from time immemorial; but there was a prejudice against it and it was not common. Bronze continued to be used in Europe until 700 or 800 B. C. as the usual material for weapons.

The cemetery of Hallstadt, ranging from 800 to 300 B. C., gives us a chronicle of the introduction of metals. Iron was introduced into Eastern Europe, Central Europe, and Egypt about 700 or 800 B. C. There is no evidence to show whence it was introduced; but with its coming we find the beginning of that great movement of which the founding of the city of Rome was a part. The Assyrian mounds show perfectly pure copper, which, it has been decided, came from the Caucasus.

Mr. Cornelius Stevenson exhibited three pieces of tilting armor of the last half of the sixteenth century: a volant-piece, a shoulder-piece, and an elbow-piece. He said they were used over the armor used in war. In the fifteenth century the tilting armor was made by itself. He described the combats, and said the knights always broke their lances, as a matter of course, and were almost invariably unhorsed. The sword was blunt and made of wood, and the mace was likewise of wood. If the combatants were not unhorsed they continued the fight with those weapons. They never struck below the chest. Before the middle of the fifteenth century there are no tilting suits. It is thought they tilted then in ordinary armor.

Prof. Maxwell Sommerville exhibited a marble representation of a lingam from India.

Mr. Culin exhibited a prehistoric tube (Plate XIII) made from a bone of the llama, from Tiahuanaco, Bolivia, a specimen collected by Dr. Max Uhle for the University Museum. Mr. Culin suggested that its shape seemed to indicate that it had been used for blowing snuff or tobacco smoke.

The Treasurer, Mr. Harry Rogers, presented his report for the year 1895, showing a balance of $604.64.

MARCH 5TH, 1896.

Mr. F. D. Langenheim read the following translation from the *Gartenlaube* concerning a coin in the Hockley Collection (No. 1566, Case No. 164.5²), at Memorial Hall:

"At the close of the Thirty Years' War (1650) a monster peace celebration was held in Nuremberg. It was then that a practical joker perpetrated the following: He caused a rumor to be cir-

---

* See M. Uhle, *Bulletin of Free Museum of Science and Art*, University of Pennsylvania, Vol. I, No. 4.

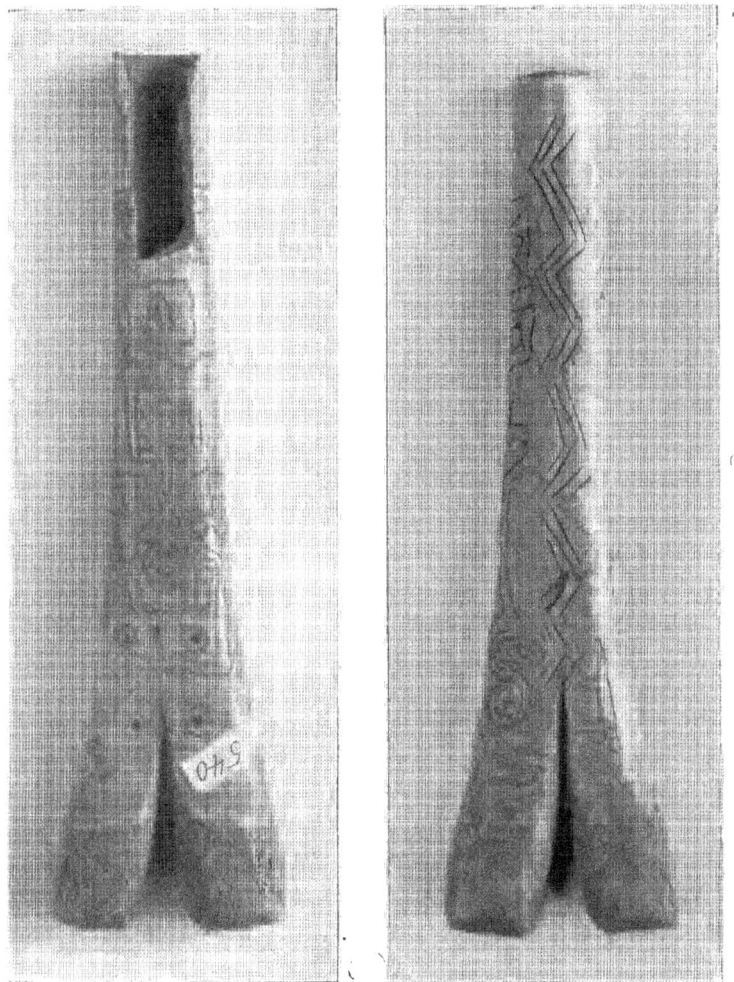

Bolivian Prehistoric Snuffing Tube.

culated in the city that on the following Sunday the Imperial Commander, the Duke Amalfi (Octavius Piccolomini), would give each lad who came to his (the Duke's) quarters, mounted on a hobby-horse, one of the so-called Peace Pfennigs (pennies). The effect of this may be imagined. From all the alleys, lanes, and by-roads of the city there came squadrons of boys mounted on hobby-horses, having only one object in view. The wooden horses neighed, and made such a noise, that the Duke hurried to the window, and there first learned the state of affairs.

"He quieted the boys with the assurance that if they came on the following Sunday, in the same manner as they had come on that day, he would attend to them. They not only came, but brought many more with them. A whole army came, fierce and defiant, and occupied in the effort to control the untamed steeds. Nuremberg was at that time the only place where such a demand for hobby-horses could have been supplied.

"The Duke presented each lad with a square silver pfennig, which he had caused to be struck with the effigy of one of the daring horsemen, as the cut shows. Contented, the mass withdrew, for a long time filling the city with their joyful shouts."— *Gartenlaube*, No. 17, 1892.

Mr. Carl Edelheim exhibited a series of Siamese coins, and presented one of them that was lacking to the Society's collection. He exhibited a Chinese gold ring with an engraved design in relief; a Japanese gold ring; a silver ring of the sixteenth century from South Germany, and another from the same place of the early seventeenth century, bearing a Madonna and child with winged angels on either side in relief.

Mr. Culin exhibited a small curved stone of polished jasper, pierced with two holes, from an Indian grave in Orange County, Florida.

Prof. Maxwell Sommerville exhibited a copper spoon used in making offerings to the gods, in India.

Mr. Charles E. Dana exhibited a pair of bellows used in the sixteenth century by ladies in powdering their hair; an Egyptian lock; a stone celt in an antler haft; a curious plumb-bob; and an old metal seal. Also, a tortoise-shell cane, captured by his father in Mexico from General Santa Ana.

It was voted that the Curator of Numismatics be authorized to transfer 91 coins to the American Philosophical Society in lieu of those which have been misplaced.

April 2d, 1896.

The death was announced of Prof. Joseph Jones. M. D., Hon-orary Vice-President of the Society for Louisiana, February 17th, 1896.

The President, Dr. D. G. Brinton, said that Dr. Jones occu-pied a chair in the Tulane University. The part of his work that came especially within the field of this Society was on the archæ-ology of Tennessee. The Smithsonian Institution published his memoir entitled *The Antiquities of Tennessee*, containing a careful investigation of the stone graves of Tennessee. In it he raised the question, not yet settled, whether syphilis existed in America before the Discovery, basing his conclusions on the lesions of the bones found in the Tennessee graves.

The death was announced of Francis C. Macauley, Cor-responding Member, at Naples, Italy, on March 16th, in the fifty-second year of his age.

President Brinton said that Mr. Macauley was deeply inter-ested in the subjects studied by our Society. He was practically the founder of the Archæological Association of the University of Pennsylvania.

President Brinton spoke of the so-called copper age in Europe, which has been assumed by some archæologists. The age of metal, he said, is divided into an age of bronze and an age of iron. The theory of a copper age, anterior to the bronze age, has been brought forward, and at present European archæologists are inclined to accept it. The theory is based upon the discovery of a large number of objects of pure copper that have been found in Europe, and that are assumed to have preceded the bronze age. President Brinton dissented from this view, and pointed out that pure copper was valueless as a material for im-plements on account of its lack of hardness. Besides, in the very early Babylonian records, we find mention of the mixture of tin and copper to produce bronze for the weapons of the gods. He concluded from the evidence adduced that the copper age is an unnecessary and impossible one

A question of Mr. Cornelius Stevenson led to a discussion on the antiquity and distribution of the sling. President Brinton said that no sling-stones, recognized as such, had been found among paleolithic remains; and he appealed to the members present to verify his assertion from their own knowledge. He said there was no instance of the use of the sling among American tribes north of Mexico.

Mr. Culin said that sling-stones and a fragment of leather, thought to be a portion of a sling, had been identified by Mr. Cushing in the Cliff Dweller Collection from Mancos Cañon, Colorado, in the University Museum.

Mr. John T. Morris spoke of the use of the sling in Egypt by the boys, to scare birds from the grain fields. Their slings are extremely well made. He had observed them on a former visit; but last winter could see none of them.

Mr. Culin mentioned the bolas in the collection recently received by the University Museum from Dr. Max Uhle, who is collecting in Peru and Bolivia. They consist of three balls fastened with rawhide thongs. Although one such implement was obtained from a grave and was, doubtless, of considerable antiquity, it was still a practicable weapon. Another had one ball of stone with two others of wood.

Mr. Culin spoke also of additional collections made by Dr. Uhle at and near Tiahuanuco. Eighteen boxes, his last consignment, have just been opened at the University. They contained many objects of extreme beauty and interest; among them, two ceremonial tablets of slate were exhibited by Mr. Culin. One, perfect, bore a face surrounded by rays, like the sun, in a rectangular depression on the surface of the tablet. It was further ornamented with small beads of copper inserted in the stone. The other tablet was one-half of a similar object.

Mr. John T. Morris exhibited an old tenon (for a mortise) inscribed with a cartouche, once used to fasten stones together in an Egyptian temple; also a carved wooden leg of a chair or throne, the lower part representing a human figure; also a box of painted wood containing a number of painted wooden statuettes. He said they were images of children who died in infancy.

Mr. Charles E. Dana exhibited two very beautiful silver coins of ancient Syracuse, and a silver coin of the Ptolemies, which he had had mounted in a gold setting at Rome.

Mr. F. D. Langenheim presented to the Society's cabinet a medal struck to commemorate the twenty-fifth anniversary of the siege of Metz, made of cannon captured from the French. The proceeds of the sale of the medal go to a fund to decorate the graves of the soldiers.

The Curator of Numismatics, Mr. F. D. Langenheim, reported

that he had made over 61 coins to the American Philosophical Society, instead of 91, since the remainder had been made up from the triplicate pieces.

President Brinton said he could not allow the occasion to pass without calling the Society's attention to the obligations it was under to its Curator of Numismatics in having successfully arranged the matter of the coins to the satisfaction of all those interested; and he cordially congratulated Mr. Langenheim.

The Chairman of the Publication Committee urged the desirableness of an early publication of the Society's Proceedings for the years 1892-95; and on his motion it was voted to appropriate $150 for the purpose, provided $100 in addition be raised by private subscription. The Publication Committee was then authorized to prepare the Proceedings of the Society from 1892 to 1895 for publication.

MAY 7TH, 1896.

The death was announced of Hamilton Disston, a Resident Member, April 30th, 1896.

The President, Dr. D. G. Brinton, exhibited the second part of Volume I of Prof. Hermann V. Hilprecht's *Old Babylonian Inscriptions*, and paid a high tribute to the importance of this valuable contribution to our knowledge of the early Babylonian inscriptions.

Mr. F. D. Langenheim exhibited a silver medal struck to commemorate the marriage of William II, Prince of Orange, and Princess Mary of England, May 12th, 1641, parents of William III, of England.

Mr. Henry Jüngerich said he had an opportunity to purchase a quantity of American half-cents for the Society's collection at a nominal price. The purchase was authorized.

OCTOBER 1ST, 1896.

The death was announced of Lewis A. Scott, of Philadelphia, Vice-President of the Society, on August 11th, 1896, in his 78th year; of Dr. G. Brown Goode, Honorary Vice-President for the District of Columbia, on September 6th, 1896; of Abel Hovelacque, of Paris, Corresponding Member; and of Isaac F. Wood, of New York, Corresponding Member.

The President, Dr. D. G. Brinton, spoke warmly in praise of Mr. Scott, and of the lamented Dr Goode. Abel Hovelacque, he said, was a man of extraordinary powers. He died comparatively young. His studies were linguistics and sociology. In sociology he made his most conspicuous mark. An avowed extremist, he took great pride in his position, and risked the sacrifice of all he might have had. He was a determined opponent of the government and an avowed and extreme atheist. He did not excite the enmity of those with whom he was thrown in contact. He was a member of the Municipal Council of the City of Paris.

President Brinton described an emblematic mound in Canada, The particulars had been communicated to him by Mr. David Boyle, the Curator of the Museum of Archæology of Toronto. The mound is in the form of a serpent; sixty feet long, eight feet across, and three feet high. The mouth was apparently open, and in front there was an oval object usually described as an egg. The discovery is without parallel so far north; although a mound exists just north of the Detroit River, not far from it. Some ethnologists attribute the construction of the mounds to the Dakotas, of the Siouan stock. According to Miss Alice C. Fletcher, they still make small mounds in front of the tepee to indicate the totem of the owner. Emblematic mounds are not confined to America, but are found in certain parts of the Old World. A French engineer described a serpent mound on the top of a flat mountain in Algeria. Mounds also occur in Australia. At the initiation of youths, a ceremony called the Bora, they threw themselves outstretched on the ground. They made a mound representing a man stretched out in this manner as a memorial of the Bora. That leads to the inquiry whether the American mounds were not likewise connected with the initiation into the gens.

Mr. Henry C. Mercer made some observations on the turkey, maize and tobacco, which the Turk, curiously enough, seems to get credit for, although all are originally American. In reference to tobacco, however, he questioned whether smoking may not have originated independently in the far East.

President Brinton answered that, so far as China is concerned, Dr. Schlegel has shown that all words connected with smoking are modern adaptations; and that tobacco was unknown until 1650, when it was introduced from Europe. Dr. Brinton traced the origin of the pipe to the tube used by the Indian medicine man to blow upon his patient. The Indians regard the soul as akin to the breath. When a man is sick and liable to die the medicine man is called in to blow upon him. In the Mayan language the very word for medicine-man is "the blower." The tubes found throughout America were all used for this purpose. No doubt, the addition of smoke, which made the breath visible, came later. The use of tobacco probably arose as a pure accident. The Indian smokes by inhalation into the lungs, producing a prompt and definite narcotic influence, the object being to bring about a condition of communion with the gods. They by no means confined themselves to tobacco: the stramonium, "jimson weed," was smoked throughout America. A powerful narcotic, it brought about a state of anæsthesia. The snake plant, and allied species, also narcotic, were used; and in Caliornia a kind of fungus, which gives rise to visions.

Mr. Inman Horner exhibited a double crown of Nuremberg; and Mr. Culin, the gold medal of the Cotton States and International Exposition at Atlanta, Georgia.

The medal and diploma awarded to the Society at the World's Columbian Exposition was formally presented. The award read as follows:

"I. Collection of American paper money. This collection consists of a series of notes from the year 1800 to 1863, which were issued by State and private banks, individuals, and corporations in the United States, many of which are from Virginia, Maryland, Delaware, Massachusetts, Mississippi, the Carolinas, Florida, Georgia, Alabama, and from the old Bank of Philadelphia. It also contains a complete collection of postal currency, issued by the United States government during the late war. It may be regarded as an interesting contribution to the financial history of the country, forming a link between the paper money of the Colonial and Continental epochs and that of the greenbacks and notes of the present time. The collection is admirably arranged and mounted in suitable frames, thus forming a handsome, interesting, and valuable collection.

"II. Collection of American historical medals. The series is formed of Washington medals; ecclesiastic and collegiate medals; military, civic and political medals, and medallic portraits of Americans, many of which are commemorative of interesting and important events in American history; also, medals of famous Americans, societies, and corporations. The Washington medals are exceptionally noteworthy, comprising many of the most famous specimens. This collection, together with that of the American paper money, exhibited by the same Society, formed a part of the exhibit of the United States National Museum at Madrid, Spain, in 1892. The collection has been admirably arranged, and is a valuable, instructive, and highly interesting exhibit. [Signed] Virginia Campbell Thompson, Individual Judge; W. F. Terry, President, Department Committee."

The Treasurer, Mr. Harry Rogers, presented his report, showing a balance of $752.05.

Mr. Westcott Bailey, of the Market Street Bridge Monument Committee, reported that the City Council had taken no action in regard to it.

NOVEMBER 5TH, 1896.

Col. Richard S. Edwards, a visitor, read a paper on "A Proposed Medal for the Philadelphia Post-Office," as follows:

A PROPOSED MEDAL FOR THE PHILADELPHIA POST-OFFICE.

BY RICHARD S. EDWARDS.

To enable you to understand the causes that brought about the existence of the medal, it may be well to outline briefly some part of the organization of the postal service in this city. You are all familiar with the main or central Post-Office at Ninth and Chestnut Streets, where the Postmaster and his administrative staff are situated, and where a general postal business is transacted. But there are also twenty-five branch post-offices, or sub-stations, scattered through the city, as far as possible in the centres of population of their respective districts. They are free-delivery offices, that is, with letter-carriers attached; and at each a regular postal business is carried on, letters are received and delivered within the district, postage stamps, postal cards, and stamped envelopes are sold, domestic and international money orders are issued and paid, and mail matter is registered. There are, besides, thirty-six receiving stations, where letters are received but not delivered, stamps, cards, and envelopes sold, mail matter registered, and domestic money-orders issued and paid; and at two of them international money orders, also, are paid and issued. Then, again, there are 146 stamp agencies, where stamps, envelopes, and cards are sold; making in all, including the central office, 208 offices embraced within the Philadelphia Postal District.

At some of the offices a very large business is transacted. At one receiving station, No. 20, in the Bourse Building, the sum received for the sale of stamps, envelopes, and cards for the year ending December 31st, 1896, amounted to $682,000. The twenty-five free delivery sub-postoffices have each a Superintendent and from one to sixty-eight letter-carriers, and from one to twenty-one clerks; with receipts from $440 to $114,113 a year. Evidently, these offices are a most important part of the postal system; and upon their good or indifferent work under their Superintendents depends in great measure the effectiveness of the whole postal system.

The present Postmaster of Philadelphia, Mr. Wm. Wilkins

Carr, has originated many reforms, improvements, and incentives to effort, but none, in my opinion, of more practical value than the plan he devised of inciting competition among the Superintendents of the twenty-five sub-stations by offering a prize to the one having the best record of management for the period from April 1st to December 31st, 1896. He decided that this prize shoud be in the nature of a token or medal that could be worn on the breast; and he appointed a committee from among the officials of the office to secure and adopt a design and have it carried into execution.

The committee, or, at least, the major part of it, was of the opinion that neither collectively nor individually did it possess any knowledge of numismatics; nor at first did it see its way very clearly, how it was to set about adopting a design for a medal without a greater knowledge of the subject. But the first step was not difficult; and designs were invited from the various business people of the city who profess to do that kind of work. A number of designs were received; but none were satisfactory. They had, however, one good effect; for they led the committee to a very clear knowledge of what was not wanted. This, though a negative condition, was a step in the right direction. It was finally determined that the prize should be in the form of a medal, and that it should symbolize the United States, the Postal Service, and the City of Philadelphia; and again designs were invited on the basis of this suggestion.

Of course, the letter-carrier was the most prominent figure among the designs sent in. For, to those unconnected with the postal service, the letter-carrier is always its representative; because he alone comes daily in contact with the public, and his gray uniform and leather satchel seem to them the visible embodiment of the whole postal service. But the fact is that, were it not for the army of faithful clerks behind the office walls, never seen nor, perhaps, heard of by the general public, though working day and night to arrange the mail in such shape that the carriers may deliver it, this later addition to the postal service, the letter-carrier, would be of no avail whatever. But here a new difficulty presented itself. Should a figure or representation of the carrier, or the railway mail clerk, or the collector, or the caser, or of any other one, or even of a reasonable number of those engaged in the different parts of the postal work, be selected, it would emphasize that branch or those branches, to the exclusion of the others; and that would manifestly be inconsistent with the idea of symbolizing the Postal Service, and not a part or parts of it. It was then determined to do away with personal representatives entirely.

While this matter was under discussion, it was discovered that one member of the committee not only possessed a knowledge of numismatics, but a very complete and thorough knowledge of it—his modesty having heretofore prevented him from disclosing that fact. It was suggested to him that he should use the national colors to represent the United States, a mail-bag for the postal service, and the Liberty Bell for the city of Philadelphia. He intimated that he might be able so to group them as to be of value as a suggestion to a professional designer. He first produced the crude design, shown with the medals; and it seemed to have so much merit that he was asked to work it out in detail and finish. As a result, the finished design, also submitted for inspection this evening, was unanimously adopted. The work was done by Mr. John B. Walters, Superintendent of Station A, at Eighteenth and Chestnut Streets; and for originality of conception, and accuracy and neatness of detail, it was, in the opinion of the committee, superior to all the designs submitted by a number of those regularly engaged in such business.

The idea of offering these medals was original with the Postmaster, and all the expense of making them was paid by him.

The medals are made from twenty-dollar gold pieces, alloyed with enough additional copper and silver, in equal weights, to reduce the gold to fourteen carats. The device is a mail-bag and the Liberty Bell on a colored ground enamelled with the national colors. The wreath upon them was carved by hand, and the laurel branches represent victory, and the oak branches strength. The mail-bag was struck up with a steel die, and is of solid gold, satin finished, and colored to represent leather. The Liberty Bell, also struck up with a steel die, is of sterling silver, and oxidized, and fastened by revels.

Col. Edwards then exhibited the three medals to be awarded in January, 1897; and they were commented on by the Society, and a discussion ensued as to the devices used to mark the post-office in other countries.

Col. Edwards referred to a diminutive post-bag used in England.

Mr. Chas. E. Dana said that generally in Europe, as, for ex-- ample, in Germany, a small horn was used. He objected that the colors, red, white, and blue on the medals were not distinctively symbolic of the United States.

Col. Edwards exhibited a small medallion containing a picture of a bird, apparently executed in feathers; and Hindoo miniatures from Agra.

Mr. Cornelius Stevenson exhibited a sword intended for use in defending fortifications, with a blade about four feet long, that slips from the end of an iron scabbard of equal length. He said it was of the sixteenth century.

Mr. Culin exhibited a collection of phallic amulets intended to ward off evil influences.

Mr. Inman Horner exhibited and presented to the Society two Japanese postage stamps, for two and five sen, issued this year in commemoration of His Imperial Highness, Prince Kitashira- kawa, lately deceased, and bearing his portrait.

Messrs. Franklin Platt, Westcott Bailey, and Inman Horner were appointed a committee to nominate officers and standing committees for the annual election at the next meeting.

DECEMBER 3D, 1896.

Mr. Culin said that his examination of certain phases of American aboriginal culture had convinced him that they showed a distinct decline, unless the early explorers or more recent observers had given misleading accounts. Or, on the other hand, the customs referred to must be regarded as reflections from a higher civilization.

The President, Dr. D. G. Brinton, summarized the evidence as to the degeneration of the Indians; and said the question was one that had occupied the attention of students, was extremely intricate, and was not to be decided affirmatively without careful consideration. At the same time, there were evidences of degeneration, both from archæological sources and in the traditions. Thus, in Yucatan, the Mayas told the earliest explorers that since the destruction of Mayapan there had been a condition of anarchy in the peninsula. Again, in Mexico is found the cemetery of Teotihuacan, the grandest ruin on the American continent, deserted and in ruins at the time of the Discovery, and vaguely attributed by the Aztecs to a race called the Toltecs. At Titicaca, in Peru, where Squier declares the stone work is unparalleled in any of the remains of Greek and Roman cities, the earliest European visitor, Cieza de Leon, found no traces of the builders; and the Indians told him that giants had once lived there. In the Ohio Valley, a country neither cultivated nor inhabited when the first white man came there, it is known there once existed a great and prosperous culture. Images almost as striking and beautiful as the famous figurines of Tanagra have been dug from the Ohio mounds, showing an artistic sentiment little removed from that of the Greeks. In all those areas there had been a culture much superior to what was found at the Discovery. Nevertheless, reasons cannot be assigned, nor can we speak of degeneracy, except in the case of Yucatan. The problem is yet unexplained, and yet unexplainable.

Mr. Inman Horner spoke of the parallel presented in Central Asia. East of the Caspian, the plain was inhabited by wandering Khirgiz, where tombs and remnants of palaces occur, built of hewn stones. All that had been said of America, he urged, would apply equally well to Central Asia.

Mr. John T. Morris called attention to the curious fact that Baalbec, with its remarkable temple, had not been mentioned in the Bible.

Mr. Horner offered the explanation that the ascendancy of Baalbec, like that of Palmyra, was commercial rather than political. Its position for a time on the great caravan route gave it temporary importance, and the piety of its rich merchants took the form of erecting columns and colonnades; but it was never a seat of empire.

Mr. Culin exhibited a series of very beautiful silver coins of the Republic of Venice, recently received by the Archæological Museum of the University of Pennsylvania from the estate of the late Francis C. Macauley. Among them were the coins of Jac. Tiepolo, 1229-1249; Renier Zeno, 1252-1268; Jac. Dandolo, 1279-1287; and Fr. Dandolo, 1328-1339.

The committee on nominations of officers and standing committees for the coming year made its report, and the whole list was unanimously elected. (See page 10.)

JANUARY 7TH.

Mr. J. Edward Farnum, a visitor, spoke of Corean coins. Money in Corea, before Europeans came there, consisted only of a large brass coin, and another of one-fifth the weight of the larger one, both called "cash" by Europeans, and marked alike, dated with the dynasty and reign; but the two sizes are readily distinguished. These old coins were pretty, and not bad for a semi-civilized people; but have now been replaced by others, and have been in great part shipped abroad, and have become rare. There are still no gold nor silver coins. On the opening of the country to Americans and Europeans, the government called for bids from the Japanese for the manufacture of similar new coins. The contractor, however, made them very roughly, chiefly of iron, but with a little copper; and twice reduced the size. Twenty pounds of the new "cash" are worth four and a half silver dollars, and a string of these coins is worth about twelve cents. At length, by a bold stroke of debasement of the coin, the king decreed that the Coreans should accept one cash in lieu of five. Hence, in northern Corea 700 cash are worth one dollar; but in the south, owing to the less submissive character of the inhabitants, 3,500 cash are worth one dollar. The silver dollar, or Japanese yen, though in use at the treaty port of Genzan, was totally uncurrent, and its value in cash wholly unknown, even to hotel-keepers at a distance of only seven miles. To illustrate the buying power of the "cash," and at the same time the honesty of the Corean peasant, it was mentioned that a fine Mongolian pheasant was bought for four and a half cents' worth of the new coins; and then the seller ran a long distance after the purchaser to return two cash that, on careful counting, had been found to be in excess. Mr. Farnum presented to the Society a number of the coins, strung upon a cord of leather.

He had traveled across the country from Seoul to Genzan. He

found the people physically very fine, averaging five feet ten inches in height, splendid men, brave and very strong. A porter, a picked man, to be sure, under promise of reward, carried a five-hundred pound bale of silk half a mile up hill. The ordinary load for a porter is one hundred pounds. But the race seems degenerate in civilization. The art of pottery is almost lost, and modern porcelain is rare; but pieces of porcelain five hundred years old are found.

Mr. Farnum had also traveled in Southeast Africa; and he exhibited a horn snuff-spoon from Zululand. The snuff is made from a narcotic weed, similar to Indian hemp, mixed with tobacco. He also exhibited a Manika-land carved snuff-bottle made of buffalo horn. The bottle is carried in a large hole made in the lobe of the ear; and that is the common way of carrying various small articles. He also exhibited two specimens of a wooden oblate-ellipsoidal, or decidedly flattened spheroidal, ball, about the size of a small apple, say two and a half inches in its larger diameter, somewhat carved and ornamented with colors; and considered by the native men of that part of Africa to be quite an indispensable, and for comfort, decency, and propriety the only essential article of dress, and thought requisite even when European dress is adopted. In the centre of one of the flattened sides of the spheroid there is a cavity about three-quarters of an inch in diameter and of about equal depth, slightly tapering inwards, said to be gauged by the size of the wearer's thumb. The ball is worn upon the end of the penis, and serves as a protection against injury in walking through the brush.

Mr. Inman Horner spoke of a similar custom in the Solomon Islands, where a shell is used in like manner.

Mr. John T. Morris spoke of the currency he had found in use in India. In addition to silver rupees, bank bills were used; but the Bombay bank bills were used only as far east as Allahabad, and were at a discount in Calcutta. He remarked upon the absence of gold coins as currency, and that even British sovereigns were not current.

Mr. Horner explained that, though gold was not current there as coin, and not, as silver is, legal tender, no more than diamonds and rubies, yet it could, doubtless, be sold to jewellers or goldsmiths. He cited Tavernier's experience in finding the native jewellers skilled at appreciating the adulteration of gold coins.

Mr. Farnum said he had been told in India that, for hoarding, the American twenty-dollar gold coin was preferred even to the British sovereign, and was taken at a premium of six per cent. The sovereign was not guaranteed full weight, and was more likely to be worn; while that American coin was always of full weight. Moreover, red gold was much preferred to yellow, and the Australian sovereign, more common in India, was very yellow.

Mr. Morris spoke of the gold mohur as not rare in India among hoarded coin, in 1890; and it was then easily procured, for example, by a certain physician, who ordinarily took a gold sovereign as a fee, but on a simple request could have a mohur instead. In 1895, however, Mr. Morris found the mohur had become very scarce.

Mr. Horner remarked that the importation of gold into India was considerable.

Mr. Morris spoke of the beauty of the silver rupee still coined at Lucknow.

Mr. Morris exhibited four specimens of the porcelain gambling counters of Siam, dating from about 1800; but whether in use now or not, he did not know.

Mr. Morris also exhibited a sacred mummified hawk from Luxor, Egypt.

Mr. F. D. Langenheim presented a white-metal medal commemorating a visit of several lodges of Philadelphia Free Masons to the City of Mexico in 1893, or thereabouts.

The Treasurer, Mr. Harry Rogers, reported on the finances of the Society, showing a balance of $741.10 on hand at the beginning of 1897.

Thanks were unanimously voted for Mr. Farnum's communications of this evening and for his gift of Corean coins.

FEBRUARY 4TH, 1897.

Mr. Culin read a letter from Thomas J. Collins, of Haddonfield, N. J., saying that Dr. R. C. Kendall, of Troy, Bradford County, Pa., has a stone phallus, one of two found along the creek bottom after a flood.

The President, Dr. D. G. Brinton, said that he knew of no aboriginal objects resembling phalli found on the Atlantic Coast, but that, on the other hand, they are extremely abundant in Central America.

After discussion, it was suggested that Mr. Culin communicate
with Mr. Collins, and ask if the phallus could be submitted for
the Society's inspection.

Mr. Lyman exhibited a Japanese sword recently presented to
the Archæological Museum of the University by Dr. D. B.
McCartee, of Tokio. It was presented to Dr. McCartee about
twenty years ago, on his retirement from his professorship in
the University at Tokio, by Mr. K. Takahashi, one of his pupils,
a bright and faithful student, now Chief Secretary to the Cabinet
of the Imperial Government, and formerly principal editor of
the official gazette. Mr. Takahashi said the sword had been in
his family for three hundred years. It looks old, and is worn
quite narrow by repeated grinding. There is no inscription on
the tang. The grooves of the blade run far along the tang, and
the tang has three holes for the *mekugi* (or rivet that holds the
hilt on), one of them very close to the outer end of the tang.
The sword seems, therefore, to have been shortened from the
length of a *katana* proper (30 to 33 inches) to that of an
ippouzashi (single sword worn by tradesmen and farmers, and
between the *katana* and *wakizashi* in length, or, say, about
25 inches long). The blade, owing to some exposure to damp-
ness on the way from Japan, is at present much tarnished and
rusty; so that it is difficult to judge of its quality.

Mr. Cornelius Stevenson exhibited the end of a pommel of a
saddle of the sixteenth century. He described it as the piece
fastened to the pommel.

President Brinton made a communication on the anthropological aspect of North Africa.

MARCH 4TH, 1897.

Mr. Charles E. Dana spoke of his efforts to investigate the seal
of Penn's charter; and read a communication from the English
Public Record Office, saying: "There are no impressions of the
Privy Seal amongst the records relating to royal grants made
in the reign of Charles II preserved in this office." The various
stages gone through by letters-patent similar to Penn's were
minutely described. "There is no trace," the letter said, "of the
seal's having been pendant or affixed to the face of any of these
documents." A dummy accompanying the papers showed the
exact manner of affixing the seal. No examples appear to

survive. Inquiry was made at the British Museum without result.

In the discussion that followed, Mr. G. Albert Lewis pointed out the amusing error of a seal of the reign of Victoria attached to the charter held in the hand of the new City Hall statue of Penn.

Mr. Dana said that the seal given in the frontispiece of *The Archives of Pennsylvania* as the one on the charter is really the great seal of the State of New York in the time of George II. He said that the arms of England change in almost every reign, and from any given arms the reign can generally be determined.

Mr. Inman Horner exhibited a valuable and perfect suit of Japanese armor lent by Mr. A. M. Hance. A discussion followed as to the origin of this peculiar defensive armor and its probable affinities with the bone plate armor of northern Japan and its possible origin therein.

President Brinton combated the view held by Prof. Otis T. Mason, that there was evidence of transference in the existence of this armor on both sides of Bering Straits, and said it might well have been an independent invention. Armor consisting of metal plates, interwoven with cords, occur in European defensive arms.

Mr. Cornelius Stevenson exhibited the following Japanese swords: a small *tantô*, originally a longer sword, cut down by regrinding, and supposed to be a Masamune; a *tachi* by Yukumitsu; a *katana*, with an exquisite lacquered scabbard, by Ikesada; a *tachi* by Yakemitsu.

Mr. Harry Rogers exhibited a number of specimens of American gold coinage, including a $2.50 and a $5.00 Bechtel piece of North Carolina, a private mint-piece of Baldwin & Co., a piece coined from the first Pike's Peak gold, etc.

Mr. Lyman exhibited a piece of Japanese rebel paper money, one yen, produced in 1877 in Kiushiu, made of blue starched cotton.

Mr. Culin exhibited several Japanese silver coins belonging to Mr. Emlen Meigs, together with a Japanese work in which the pieces were illustrated.

The Curator of Numismatics. Mr. F. D. Langenheim. reported that he had purchased the proof-set of United States coins for the current year, to be placed in the cabinet.

It was voted that the Committee on Numismatics report on the question of securing the mint medals.

APRIL 1ST, 1897.

Mr. John T. Morris exhibited two Japanese fire-locks, one inlaid with the badge of the Tokugawa family; and an old Indian fire-lock from Delhi.

Mr. Cornelius Stevenson exhibited a German fire-pistol for striking a light.

Mr. Culin exhibited a pair of boxing gauntlets embroidered with gold thread, used by Russian nobles in combats in the last century. With them there was a true cestus, capable of a fatal blow. The tops of the gauntlets were inlaid with red leather, and had a text stamped in gold letters around the edge.

Mr. Culin also exhibited an old copper horn, the property of Mr. Charles H. Bockius, to whom it had been given by a Jew about sixty years old. The Jew said it had been given to him by his grandfather, who called it an old Israelitish horn. It was pronounced to be an old German hunting horn.

MAY 6TH, 1897.

The death of Justo Zaragosa, of Madrid, Corresponding Member, was announced.

Dr. Max Uhle, a visitor, exhibited and discussed a quipu that he had brought from Bolivia. It is said by von Tschudi that in the Puna of Bolivia quipus are still used in the way so important in ancient times, when it would not have been possible to administer the empire without them. Another finer specimen than the present one was sent by Dr. Uhle to Berlin from Challaai, the island in the southern side of Lake Titicaca. The quipus are now used by the Indians for rendering account to the owners of plantations (haciendas) concerning the product of the fields. The Indians do not like to show the quipus to the whites. The present specimen belonged to an Indian of Cutusuma, who had been an alcalde. At the close of the year he had to give account of the shepherds to the next following alcalde. On one side the sheep are represented. The knots are of different sizes, large and small. Three of them represent hundreds; eight are for tens; and seven small ones are for units: making in all 387. There is also a thread for keeping a separate account of sheep eaten. On another string the knots represent 285 sheep. The knots of another string show the number of increase of young animals, 85. On the quipu sent to Berlin the males were represented by knots in a brown string, and the females by knots in a white string. There were keepers of the quipus, who correspond to our book-keepers, and who count them up to 100,000. The Indians, how-ever, are now very poor, and though they probably know the use of the quipus from perfectly maintained traditions, they have too little property to require the use of them. (Dr. Uhle dis-cusses the subject more fully in the *Bulletin* of the Museum of Science and Art, University of Pennsylvania, Vol. I, No. 2, Dec., 1897.)

He spoke also of the slings used by the Bolivian Indians. The designs on the cords of the slings differ according to the tribes. They always go about with the slings, and also use them in battle. On the second of December, at Santa Barbara, they go out and fight, and on one such occasion broke the bones of six men.

Mr. Lyman exhibited a recent pamphlet, *Decorations of Swords and Sword Furniture*, by Edward Gilbertson, with very interesting and beautiful illustrations of Japanese sword decorations.

Mr. Culin exhibited a Corean name tablet.*

OCTOBER 6TH, 1897.

The death was announced of Hon. J. Hammond Trumbull, Honorary Vice-President of the Society, for Connecticut, August 5th, 1897, aged 75 years; and of J. Sergeant Price, Vice-Presi-dent, August 16th, 1897, aged 66 years; Achille Postalacca, of Athens, Greece, Corresponding Member (President of the Numismatic Society of Athens), died in 1897.

The President, Dr. D. G. Brinton, said Dr. J. Hammond Trum-bull was one of the best bibliographers we had, one who devoted his whole life to the studies we are interested in; and he left one of the largest collections of books in existence in reference to the Algonquin languages. Mr. J. Sergeant Price, a son of

---

* See *Bulletin of Free Museum of Science and Art*, Vol. I, No. 1.

the former President of our Society, always took an active interest in its welfare, and, whenever the Society desired to extend itself and asked for financial aid, was ready with assistance.

Mr. Culin read a communication from Mr. Charles Laubach, of Riegelsville, Bucks Co., Pa., giving an account of the stove plates manufactured at Durham Furnace, Durham, Pa., from 1741 to 1789.

Iron stoves were unknown before 1678, when Prince Rupert, of England, attempted to convert a fireplace into a furnace. This was the first attempt to force smoke back over the fire and create heat for warming apartments by the aid of iron. Early in the eighteenth century, about 1710, Count Polignac, of France, made an attempt to convert an ordinary fireplace into a heating apparatus by simply constructing a fireplace with an iron back, hearth, and jambs. The result was only a slight saving of heat. In 1716 Dr. Desaguliers, of London, succeeded in improving the Polignac fireplace so that it could be used for burning coal.

The first attempt at manufacturing heating apparatus at Durham, Pa., was in 1741, by the Durham Furnace Company. The firm consisted of George Taylor (later one of the signers of the Declaration of Independence), James Logan and James Morgan, iron masters (the latter being the father of General Daniel Morgan, the hero of Cowpens).

The 1741 stove pattern was called the "Adam and Eve," from its embellishment. It was in the form of a box, two feet square, without side or oven doors, having merely one door in front to supply it with fuel and draft, and a hole on top to allow the escape of smoke. The stove was designed by its inventor to instruct as well as to supply comfort, having inscribed in raised characters the date 1741, surrounded with fine scroll work. Above this were raised figures representing Adam and Eve, the serpent, several fruit trees, and a variety of animals in the background. In 1745 Franklin invented the famous stove which bears his name. This pattern continued to be cast at the Durham Furnace until 1774, and probably later.

In 1756, when the furnace was leased and operated by Captain Flowers and James Morgan, a new design of stove was invented by the firm and cast at the furnace. The side plates were highly embellished with scroll work and the following inscription:

"DIS · IST · DAS ·· JAHR · DA ·   1756."

In 1774, when George Taylor, Samuel Williams, and James Morgan were the members of the firm operating the Durham Furnace, a new model of a stove was constructed with the inscription: "Durham Furnace, 1774." This was surrounded by a wealth of fine scroll work. A portion of a stove with the above inscription and the date thereon was for many years placed in a conspicuous position in front of the Easton, Pa., post-office.

In 1779 Richard Backhouse became proprietor of the Durham Iron Works. During the Revolution he supplied Washington's army with shot, cannon-balls, canister and grape. At the close of the war he commenced the manufacture of stills, steel wagon springs, stoves, and stovepipes, in addition to pig and bar iron. In 1785 he invented an improved ten-plate stove, constructed with stovepipe attachment, as at that time stovepipe was considered a luxury. In 1789 the Valentine Eckert pattern stove was largely cast here and at the Sally Ann Furnace, near Allentown, Pa. Captain Valentine Eckert, of Revolutionary fame, had, in the year 1789, a neat model of a stove constructed, which was largely cast at Durham and at the Allentown and Reading furnaces. The stove bore the inscription, "Valentine Eckert, Sally Ann Furnace," scroll work and the American eagle, carrying the motto "E Pluribus Unum" in its mouth. It is curious to note, according to the Durham Furnace ledgers, that the various stove patterns—Adam and Eve, 1741; Franklin, 1745; Philadelphia, 1755; Captain Flowers and Morgan, 1756; George Taylor, 1774; Mount Pleasant, 1780; Richard Backhouse, 1785; Captain Eckert, 1789, and Pettibone, 1781—were frequently exchanged among the various furnaces and forges in Pennsylvania and New Jersey, and cast at designated furnaces to supply the needs and tastes of the inhabitants of the surrounding region.

In the discussion that followed, Mr. Inman Horner referred to the furnace plates which it was customary to put on iron blast furnaces, giving the date of their erection; and said he hoped to exhibit such a plate at the next meeting of the Society.

President Brinton read a letter from a gentleman at Utica, N. Y., who asked for information about certain curved stone implements, and gave a sketch of three such objects from different parts of the United States. After discussion, it was concluded that such objects might have been used by the Indians as fish hooks, but that many are forgeries, created to meet the demands of collectors for relics of striking and unusual form.

Mr. Culin exhibited a copy of the *Galerie Américaine du Musée d'Ethnographie du Trocadéro*, Part I, recently presented to the Museum of Science and Art of the University of Pennsylvania by the Duke de Loubat.

President Brinton said that this very beautiful publication was due to the generosity of the Duke de Loubat, and was the work of Dr. E. T. Hamy, Member of the Institute, Conservator of the Ethnographical Museum of the Trocadéro. The French Government, about the time when Mexico was expected to become an ally of France, sent a number of collectors to that country, who obtained many superb antiquities, especially in the State of Chiapas. Those objects have remained in the Museum of the Trocadéro, unpublished and undisturbed for many years; until the Duke de Loubat came forward and defrayed the expense of this work. Dr. Brinton, however, had looked in vain in it for certain terra-cotta images with curved legs, which Dr. Hamy believes to show the influence of Buddhism in America. They are, however, "Lords of the Cycle." The work is a beautiful specimen of typography, and should be welcomed as a very important contribution. Dr. Brinton, when in Paris, met Mr. Pinart, by whom most of the specimens figured in the work were collected. He is a very accomplished Americanist. He has given to the town of Boulogne a collection from the northwest coast of America. Dr. Brinton visited the museum, and had the opportunity to see his very interesting and useful collection. It comprises a number of masks, more remarkable in some respects than those in the American Museum of Natural History, at New York. They are occasionally rude, and indicate an early period of art. There is also a large collection of spears and harpoons. Mr. Pinart was there in 1863 or 1864, before the active manufacture of "ancient" objects.

Mr. F. D. Langenheim exhibited two Victoria Jubilee medals, issued by private persons; a commemorative medal of the one hundredth birthday of William I. of Germany; and à commemorative medal of the eightieth birthday of Bismarck.

Mr. Culin exhibited three gold obans, and the Japanese Order of the Rising Sun, recently deposited in the Museum of Science and Art of the University of Pennsylvania by Mr. 'Joseph U. Crawford. They had been presented to him by the Japanese

Government in recognition of his work in building American railways in Japan.

November 4th, 1897.

The death was announced of Justin Winsor, Corresponding Member, October 26th, 1897, aged 66.

Mr. Inman Horner spoke of the promise he made last month to exhibit a furnace plate at this meeting. He had in mind the Batstow furnace. He had since found at that furnace, instead of three plates as he expected, only a single plate, erected at the time of building the last furnace in 1836. The plate was a large cast iron one with a simple inscription in relief.

Mr. Culin exhibited a bowl or platter game of the Tobique (Amalecite) Indians, of New Brunswick, recently collected, and presented to the Museum of the University of Pennsylvania by Geo. E. Starr, Esq., of this city. The implements for the game consist of six discs of bone or antler (apparently bone), marked with star-like decorations on one side, a platter of maple wood, and four large counting sticks and fifty small ones. Mr. Culin was now prepared to maintain that the beaver-teeth game of the Indians of the valley of the Columbia River had been transmitted from the south, and was a transformation of the cane and staff game of the more southerly Indians. In fact, upon the evidence of the specimens he had now collected, he considered all the games in which objects were tossed like dice, among the American Indians, were derived from some common centre, somewhere in the southwest, approximately in Mexico.

Mr. F. H. Cushing spoke in agreement with Mr. Culin as to the significance of the evidence of the southern or southwestern origin of the game mentioned.

Mr. Inman Horner observed that the symbolism of the game raises a very deep question, as to whether there is any identity of religious belief in all parts of the country, a natural inference from the universal existence among the Indians of a divinatory game having the same symbols.

The President, Dr. D. G. Brinton, briefly opposed Mr. Culin's conclusions.

Mr. Culin also exhibited a wampum belt, made of old shell wampum strung upon cotton cord, likewise collected by Mr. Starr from the same woman of the Tobiques, along with the other objects. The belt was six strands wide, of 96 beads to a row, but was imperfect through the removal of several beads from five rows. In the centre there was a cross made of white beads. From comparison with pictures of wampum belts in the Trocadéro Museum, known to be in part of the late Christian times and bearing Catholic texts and the like, Mr. Culin believed the belt to belong to the same period. He also exhibited some strings of wampum attached to long bone beads, such as are worn by the Sioux.

Mr. Cushing remarked that the red feathers at the ends of the strings showed that these beads had come from one of the Plains tribes, whence they had undoubtedly been traded to the East.

Mr. Culin called attention to the numerous references to the use of wampum as stakes in the tribal games. The grains mentioned as stakes by the French missionaries were wampum beads; and, again, the great stakes in the intertribal games were collars or belts of wampum, estimated, for example, by Father Lalemant as of extraordinary value. Mr. Culin believed, in fact, that the name of the Micmac game of *wobunarunk* meant nothing else but the wampum game; for *wobun* was the same word—white— as wampum.

Mr. Culin also exhibited a pottery inkstand of the last century, decorated with yellow, red, and green designs, probably made in Bucks County or Northampton County, Pa. Also, a horn penknife, with a case containing several blades and an eraser, purchased at Nazareth, Pa.; and four single-bladed iron knives of rude make, two marked on the blades with a tomahawk, purchased from an old Indian trader at Nazareth. The trader said he had got them many years ago from another trader who had had them for use in trading with the Indians.

President Brinton made an inquiry in reference to a class of archæological objects found in archæological museums of the United States that are miniature objects, too small for practical use. Prof. F. Starr, of Chicago, had recently discovered a number of these things in the Lake of Chiapas, in Mexico; and winds up his paper with the idea that they are gifts to the gods.

Mr. Cushing suggested that, as in Zuñi, these objects were intended as property-fetiches, sacrificed that they might reproduce their kind.

Messrs. Franklin Platt, Westcott Bailey, and Inman Horner

were appointed a committee to nominate officers and standing
committees for the annual election at the next meeting.

DECEMBER 2D, 1897.

Mr. Frank Hamilton Cushing, a Corresponding Member,
made a communication on the origin of the so-called "banner
stones" and "gorgets" of the American Indians.

The precise use of these stones has never been understood and
they have been vaguely classified, together with several other
varieties, as "ceremonials." By means of a beautiful series of
specimens from the University Museum, comprising part of the
well-known Brinton collection from Ohio, Mr. Cushing demon-
strated the descent of the double-winged banner-stone from the
double-bladed war axe. The idea was suggested to him by a
wooden club with double blades which he found in the muck of
an ancient key at Marco, Florida.

The double war axe, represented both in the hand and on the
head dress of the figures impressed on copper from the Etawa
mounds in Georgia, served as an intermediate link; the banner
stone, of beautifully banded slate, being the warrior's badge, carried as an axe or worn upon the breast, or used in war invoca-
tions and calumet ceremonies.

The development of the so-called gorget from the single and
double axe of war was also clearly shown, as well as the similar
origin of the much-discussed "boat-shaped stones"; and, in fact,
nearly all of the curious so-called "ceremonial" objects from the
Ohio mounds, and elsewhere, including even the famous and
mysterious "bird-shaped ornaments," were indicated by Mr.
Cushing as belonging to this war axe series, judging by the
nature of their materials and other features. He suggested the
Southern origin of these symbolic specimens, tracing them to the
extreme South, where they existed universally as practical
weapons.

At each step northward they appear to have become more and
more highly conventionalized. A most important aid in the
demonstration was a remarkable Carolina war axe, from the collection of Dr. Samuel G. Morton, recently presented to the University by Mrs. W. H. Miller.

Dr. Max Uhle followed Mr. Cushing with an exhibition of
copper axes from Peru, displaying specimens of full size and

others of the same material in miniature. He expressed his conviction that the miniature forms were sacrificial in character, analagous to the miniature slings and the breech-cloths and ponchos, of which he found specimens in many graves.

In this connection, he related the custom of the markets held by the Indians in Bolivia on the 24th of January and the 6th of August, at which all kinds of miniature objects of use were sold; the custom being explained by the belief that the purchasers insured to themselves an abundance of similar things all the year.

Mr. Cushing said that in ancient days in Zuñi a market was held by persons especially appointed, at which similar miniature objects, called the seed of property, were apportioned, not sold, for precisely the same purpose.

Dr. Uhle also said that, in his opinion, the so-called musical stones of nephrite, to which attention was first called by Humboldt, found in the Antilles, Venezuela, and along the Caribbean Sea, were to be explained on the theory expounded by Mr. Cushing. Dr. Uhle had long contested their conventional explanation.

At the conclusion of the communications, the President, Dr. Daniel G. Brinton, expressed the opinion that the identification of the stone implements marked an epoch in American archæology. He freely and unconditionally accepted Mr. Cushing's identification, opposing only the ideas of transmission from the south, which Mr. Cushing urged. An axe, similar to the Southern type, which Mr. Cushing traced northward, occurred in Egypt in the fourth and again in the twelfth dynasty, yet we could not regard it as evidence of intercourse with America.

A discussion on the reasons for the doubling of the axe followed. Mr. Inman Horner pointed out the naturalness of selecting the axe, a short weapon like the Roman sword, as a symbol of bravery. The doubled axe was the symbol of the highest bravery. Mr. Charles E. Dana called attention to the doubling of the eagle on coats of arms resulting from two coats of arms divided and placed in juxtaposition—when an eagle occurred on each, they formed together a double eagle. Mr. Cushing said that among the Pueblos the doubling of the war axe was often precisely for the reason given by Mr. Dana. When an animal was drawn with two heads it was with the idea that the potency of its two eyes might be effective.

Mr. Cornelius Stevenson exhibited two Italian daggers of the sixteenth century, of exquisite workmanship, obtained by him on his recent visit to Europe. One, a *main gauche*, had holes near the hilt to catch and break the adversary's sword. The other, of silver inlay, from the Brett collection, had the blade pierced with small holes to receive poison.

Mr. Westcott Bailey exhibited a jubilee medal, and a forty-franc piece of 1811.

Mr. Carl Edelheim exhibited some interesting antique rings: one, old German silver, carved with Madonna and child; one, Italian silver and gilt, enamelled; one, a Burmese ring.

Special thanks were voted to Mr. Jul. Meili, of Zurich, Switzerland, for the gift of his book, *Die Münzen der Colonie Brasilien.*

It was voted "that the Committee on Numismatics be and are hereby authorized to withdraw from the collections of the Society, now on deposit in Memorial Hall, such coins, medals, and other objects in duplicate as they may see fit, for the purpose of selling or exchanging the same: *Provided,* however, that this resolution shall not apply to the withdrawal of the collection as a whole, nor repeal the resolution passed April 5th, 1894, depositing the same."

The Curator of Numismatics, Mr. F. D. Langenheim, reported the following gifts of coins to the Society for its collection from Mr. J. Colvin Randall: a Columbian half-dollar, 1893; an Isabella quarter-dollar, 1893; an uncirculated half-dime, 1853. Likewise, from Mr. L. J. Sutton: eleven silver, one nickel, and three copper coins. The Curator also reported that Mr. Randall had given six perfect pieces in exchange for six perforated ones in the Society's collection in Memorial Hall.

The Nomination Committee reported the list of nominations for officers and standing committees for the coming year. (See page 11.)

JANUARY 6TH.

The President, Dr. Daniel G. Brinton, briefly reviewed the history of the Society during the past forty years, as it was just forty years since the foundation of the Society. He then delivered an address on the subject of "Glacial Man," and recounted the discoveries in that direction during the past few years in both the Old World and the New.

Mr. Inman Horner then made the presentation of a medal to the President in a brief speech. He referred to the distinguished services Dr. Brinton had performed for science, and to the signal ability with which he had presided over the Society during the past fifteen years. The medal was to be afterwards made, and was now tendered to the President as an expression of admiration and esteem and in recognition of his services by the members of the Society.

President Brinton made answer to Mr. Horner's speech, and thanked him and the Society for the compliment they had conferred.

Mr. Horner exhibited a pair of Chinese scales, used in weighing silver, and a "shoe" of silver, used in China as money; and a modern Japanese gold piece of the value of five dollars; all collected by Messrs. Geo. L. and J. Edward Farnum on their recent trip to the East.

Mr. Cornelius Stevenson exhibited a Louis XIV sword, inlaid with gold.

Mr. Culin exhibited some remarkable jade objects from Costa Rica, recently loaned to the University Museum.

FEBRUARY 3D.

The death of Henry Thayer Drowne, a Corresponding Member, on December 10th, 1897, was announced.

The President, Dr. D. G. Brinton, spoke further on the alleged discovery of relics of glacial man in America. He pointed out that Dr. Henry B. Kümmel, in *Science*, January 28th, 1898, had shown that the relics found near Trenton occurred in what is probably wind-blown sands that were decidedly post-glacial and partly modern, with some apppearance of stratification, but not real stratification; and that the human implements were, no doubt, laid down by Indians at the time the sand was deposited. It is not impossible that some pieces of stone may occur even in such wind-blown sand; and some pieces may have been lifted up by the roots of falling trees. The layer in question is only four or five feet thick. Also, men might have carried boulders along the river side. The conclusion, then, was drawn that the sand was later than the glacial gravel, and contemporaneous with man, and strictly modern. This, President Brinton said, was the final blow at the twenty-five-year-old theory of the existence of glacial man in the Trenton gravel. Still, we may yet find him elsewhere; in caves, for example; as he did probably exist in America during glacial times. It appears, however, not to be true that man's remains have been found in glacial deposits near Trenton, but only in a deposit that may be no more than 1,000 or 2,000 years old.

Mr. Edelheim exhibited a fragment of a tile from the Alhambra, with remarkably brilliant coloring. The clay, reddish in color, appeared to him similar to what is found in Persia; and he thought the tile was, perhaps, made in Arabia and brought by the Moors to Spain.

He also exhibited a painting on glass, perhaps seven inches by four, probably one of twelve representing the Apostles, by Martin Schongauer; and pointed out that the glass had been covered on both sides with varnish and then etched on the varnish, not on the glass, making the picture perfect on both sides, but especially so on one side; and that a brush had been used to add tones, in order to make the etched figure perfectly plastic; and that strong heat had been used.

Mr. Stevenson exhibited a peculiarly constructed engraved Mexican flint-lock "powder-tester" of this century, that had been given to him by Dr. Donaldson Smith.

Mr. Horner exhibited a medal that had apparently been presented by Napoleon III to old soldiers, survivors of the Grande Armée. The date of striking the medal was not given; but it bore the words: "St. Helena, 5 May, 1821," and "1792-1815."

He also exhibited a medal from a small town in Austria, a gold or gilt coin in the centre, bearing a representation of St. Michael and the dragon, and a curious coat of arms.

JAPANESE SWORDS.

CHIEFLY BY EDWARD GILBERTSON

FEBRUARY 23D, 1898.

A special meeting of the Society was held this evening in conjunction with the Mining and Metallurgical Section of the Franklin Institute.

Captain E. L. Zalinski, of New York, read a paper on Japanese swords, and exhibited seventy-two fine specimens of them, a small part of his collection of the work of celebrated masters. He briefly described the Japanese method of forging swords, and gave some of his experiences in collecting them.

Mr. Lyman, by way of discussing the subject, spoke of Edward Gilbertson, Esquire, of Ilfracombe, in Devonshire, England, and read extracts from Mr. Gilbertson's private letters of the past four years. He is not only the leading English collector of Japanese swords and mounts, but is extremely well informed and a very intelligent and careful student of his specimens, with much acute observation, and not a mere collector of curiosities. He has done a great deal to encourage the study of Japanese art, and especially was for that purpose one of the founders of the Japan Society of London; and he now rejoices to see it very successful, with a membership of over 600, and the number of collectors and the demand for Japanese objects largely and rapidly increased. He also finds much pleasure in displaying and explaining his own collection of over 260 swords and other Japanese objects to interested visitors, and is constantly adding to it, and revising and regrouping his catalogue of it. His own thorough study and careful criticism of these objects has resulted in an admirable paper on the "Decoration of Swords and Sword Furniture," published by the Japan Society in 1894, with beautiful illustrations from his collection; and a few weeks ago he communicated to the same Society a paper on sword blades, which has not yet reached us in print.*

One very interesting subject mentioned in this recent paper is the prehistoric sword blade. In a letter of last December, he

---

* Read November 24th, 1897, and published in the *Transactions of the Japan Society*, Vol. IV.

says: "The paper was already too long, otherwise I should have liked to say more about the earliest blades; for I am convinced that the two-edged *tsurugi* is not the original form of the Japanese sword. Without an exception, I think, every blade found in the dolmens and burial mounds is a single-edged weapon and perfectly straight. The *shiri ken* and *shichiyô ken* are of that form, but engraved, and one has a hilt bound round with copper wire. These are possibly of a somewhat later date than those of the dolmens; although all of these last are, I think, too much oxidized to enable one to judge whether they are engraved or not. The dolmen swords had tsubas, ovoid, of iron or of copper plated with gold, and pierced; some with scabbards of embossed copper, with broad silver bands, and with rings for suspending them—corresponding completely with the *tachi* or *katana*. But I have seen no representation or description of a suspended *tsurugi*, two-edged; although, I fancy, they must have been suspended, and that they were introduced from China or Corea. Nor can I believe that the *katana* was invented by Amakuni, by dividing the *tsurugi;* for, certainly, the dolmen blades were made hundreds of years before his time."

Later, March 16th, 1898, he kindly encloses two extracts from his manuscript catalogue of his swords, discussing prehistoric swords and *nagatachi* as follows:

"The original form of the Japanese sword is always stated to be the *tsurugi* or *ken*, a two-edged straight weapon, the two names being merely the Japanese and the Chinese rendering of the same character. There are two forms of the *ken*, the earlier having a point broader than the base of the blade, and forming a very obtuse angle, the later being of equal length from hilt to point, the latter formed by two curves. Japanese writers also tell us that the *katana*, or single-edged sword, was invented by Amakuni, who lived about A. D. 700, by dividing the *ken* longitudinally. I can find nothing that supports these statements, but, on the contrary, all my evidence goes to show that both of them are erroneous.

"Burial mounds and dolmens abound in Japan, and many hundreds have been opened, Mr. Gowland having examined 400. In them he found, among other things, swords, several of which are in the British Museum; and others, derived from various sources, are to be found preserved in private collections or temple treasuries, in Japan. All of these, so far as I can learn, are without exception single-edged straight blades—*katana*, in fact, without a single two-edged blade among them. Burial in mounds or dolmens seem to have been used in Japan from a little before the Christian era to about the year 600, or 700 at the latest; so it is absurd to credit Amakuni with the invention of a form of blade in use hundreds of years before he was born. I have representations of three blades bearing his signature. One of them is similar to the dolmen blades; the others are of the ordinary *katana* form, narrower at the point than at the base and slightly curved, a form impossible to obtain by dividing either kind of *ken;* and I take the truth to be that he probably first made *katana* of the modern shape.

"The earliest example of the *ken* that I can hear of is the *tamakazari* sword of the Emperor Shomu, who died in 751; and it is preserved in the Shoso-in at Nara. It is described in the list of presentations to the temple of Todaiji, under the date of the 6th month of the 8th year of Tempei Shoho (A. D. 736), as 'one large *Chinese* sword adorned with gold and silver; length of blade, 2 *shaku*, 6 *sun*, 4 *bu* (31½ inches), two-edged, the hilt covered with *same,*' etc., etc. I doubt much whether the *ken* was ever very much used in Japan, except for short blades, among which it is frequently found.

"I can learn nothing about the *nagatachi*, or 'long *tachi,*' several examples of which exist in England, one of them being in my own collection, and several others are preserved in various temple treasuries in Japan. One, at the temple of Gongen, at Oji, has a blade four feet one inch long, with a tang two feet one inch, implying a total length from the pommel to the end of the scabbard of about seven feet three inches. That of Noritsune, at Itsukushima, made by Yukiyoshi, has a blade four feet eight and a half inches in length, weighing fourteen pounds; and another blade at the same place is seven feet three inches long from the pommel to the end of the scabbard. My own has a blade four feet two and a half inches long, the total length being six feet two inches, made by Fujiwara Hiromoto in 1838, the year of the accession of the Shógun Iyetoshi; but it has no *mon* connecting it with him

"It seems clear to me that none of these could ever have been used as weapons. They require two men to draw them, and although a strong man might wield them, mine, at least, is so ill-balanced that it would be a most inconvenient weapon; for an active opponent could easily run within the guard of a man using such a sword, making him practically defenceless. My own conviction is, that they were merely processional swords, borne before or after the Shôgun or great daimios on certain occasions, more especially as their style of mounting is that belonging to commanders. I ought, however, to state that the *Kogeishirio* says, unless the interpreter has given me an incorrect translation, that one of these *nagatachi*, seven feet four inches long, was *worn* by a member of the Fukuma family. This would nullify my theory, but I still doubt the correctness of that statement. I cannot conceive it to be probable that any man would go into battle with a weapon of that length dangling in front of him. He could only hold the scabbard, while some one else drew his sword for him; and, when that was held by him, he would be encumbered by about five feet of heavy and useless scabbard."

One of the principal new points mentioned by Mr. Gilbertson, in his recent paper, appears to be the remarkable skill shown by the sword grinders and sharpeners in giving final shape to the sword, a matter that he has several times discussed in his private letters. For example, he wrote, last September: "One very interesting feature in *katana* blades, long ones especially, is the truth of the curve, more particularly when it is a blade having a '*sori*' [bend] of an inch, or an inch and a quarter." Again, last December, he speaks of "the astonishing truth and accuracy of the lines and curves. In the *katana* which tapers towards the point, I find the edge, the line defining the *shinogi* [parallel flat surfaces] and *jigane* [sloping surfaces] and the back all curves, not parallel, but all true, and preserving from hilt to point their proportional distances. This is not an easy matter to do on paper, but to do it on a flat stone, with one part of the *jigane* intensely hard, and the other comparatively soft, is to me a surprising piece of skill; for the natural tendency is to make a hollow at the soft side of the flat." In November, 1895, he wrote: "Numbers of my blades are a pleasure to me to look at merely on account of the grinding, knowing how it is done. The faces are as truly flat, the lines as perfect, and the long, delicate curves as true as if they were lines drawn by a machine. I had a great triumph once over a man who maintained that any good English workman could do it. He was one of the great furniture makers, and I asked him if any of his men could do it in wood.

'Hundreds,' he replied. So I gave him a blade, about twenty-five inches long, and showed him that the lines and curves were mathematically true, the *shinogi* and *jigane* perfectly straight and level by a straight edge in every part. I told him if one of his men would make me a copy of the blade, not shorter, that would stand the same tests, I would give the man a couple of sovereigns. Four days afterward the blade came back, and the son of the gentleman told me that two of their men tried it, and brought what looked like an exact copy, but, on testing it, it was untrue. The second man, after hours spent in endeavoring to get the lines true, after having got the faces true, burst into a fit of swearing that was terrific, broke the thing up and dashed it on the floor. It beat the French sword makers, Colonel LeClerc said, with all their scientific appliances."

In a letter of January, 1896, he says: "I find that the Japanese sword is a subject that always surprises people not familiar with its details. To me there are still many mysteries, as it were, connected with it, that only explain themselves very gradually. You mention the coating the steel bar with clay, etc., before it is put into the fire, every time it is going to be folded and welded. In bringing it up to the welding heat, I fancy the coating must be burned into bricklike material, and that it must be a difficult matter to get rid of this perfectly, before the bar gets dangerously cold. Unless it were all removed perfectly, there would be sand cracks and defects fatal to the quality of the blade, and to the exquisite grain that characterizes the fine blades.

"Then there is the tempering, and I am inclined to think that, after all, that was the secret of all the famous *kotô* [old sword] smiths; for as to forging, grinding, and finishing, I can conceive nothing superior to some of the modern blades that I have, or some with false signatures of the great smiths. There was not only the composition of the protective coating, but there was the knowledge—a sort of instinct—that enabled the smith to detect the exact moment when the bared edge was at the proper temperature. Doubtless, the temperature of the water was a great part, and whether it was pure water, and also the mode of plunging the blade into it."

In September, 1897, he writes: "I came across, in one of my Japanese books on swords, a passage describing the process of curving or straightening blades. The former was done by hammering it on both sides from hilt to point, the latter by applying a piece of heated copper to the back (*mune*) until the *shinogi* became purple, and then putting it, edge first, into water, repeating the process until the desired curve is obtained; and this is more readily achieved with hard blades than with others. In connection with that, I found that the Osafune, Bizen, work between 1375 and 1427 was called *ko-sori-mono*, from the *sori*—that is, the depth of the curve—being small."

In August, 1896, he says: "In the *Kotô Meidzukushi* I found a puzzle cleared up. As you must have noticed, the *kotô* [old sword] smiths did not shine in the way of calligraphy in signing their tangs; and I found occasionally blades with the names of eminent smiths in gold damascening, the characters well formed, but utterly unlike their engraved autographs. Some even were written in red lacquer on the tang. Now, I found from the *Kotô Meidzukushi* that the *mekiki*, the experts, often, when they certified an unsigned blade as being by an eminent master, put his signature upon it in damascening, sometimes adding their own, as in the case of a Masamune of mine, where the *mekiki* Hon-a has put his own name and *kakihan* [monogram] on the other side. But this addition of the signature in damascening is mentioned in the *orikami* [expert's certificate]. The work of the old Gotos, who never signed their work, was certified in the same way, chiefly, I think, by one of the later Gotos, Mitsumori, or others about his time. I now think that *kotô* blades that I have, with the signatures in red lacquer, or *zôgan* [damascening], evidently not by the man to whom they are assigned, have probably had *orikami* certificates attached to them that have been lost. Hütterott speaks only of the Honami family as experts, Koyetsu dating back to the sixteenth century, and another Honami being the sword-sharpener—one of their functions—to the present Emperor. But my *orikami* and three others that I have seen, of the seventeenth and eighteenth centuries, are decidedly signed 'Hon-a,'—only two characters. I have never seen a certificate by one of the Honami and wonder if there is any connection between the two families. My Hon-a is of 1818." A scholarly Japanese in Philadelphia thinks that the two families probably had a common ancestry.

Of his own extremely useful labors and of his collection, Mr. Gilbertson says, in his letter of October 6th, 1895: "I have five [Japanese] works, in about forty volumes, which contain full-sized representations of tangs, points, etc., and short or long notices of smiths. Some are arranged according to the Iroha, others by provinces, others by families; so that it is a very troublesome affair to hunt up any given man, if one wants to compare a signature, *yakiba*, *yasuriye*, or the end of a tang. So I have been making a general index to all the volumes, arranged alphabetically, and have just completed it. [In a previous letter he had said he had made a manuscript volume of 500 pages of over 1,000 tang inscriptions.] The next thing is to copy all the tangs into one book, arranging them in the same way, with references to the originals; and then I shall be better able to distinguish two men of the same name, but of different dates, and shall have a good many absolute dates instead of 'about.' I have, however, only one authority on old swords, the *Kotô Meidzukshi;* the *Kokonkaji Meidzukushi* being mixed, and the others being all on *Shintô* [new sword] makers. . . . My collection of swords is now tolerably extensive and interesting, furnishing a good deal of material for study; and has paid me very well in the way of saving me from the temptation to buy Masamunes and other blades nominally by great masters, that have been offered to me from time to time. But some of these forgeries have let me into the knowledge of the fact that, although as temperers and makers of swords of remarkable quality these early masters are unrivalled, there are blades of the eighteenth and early nineteenth centuries that as a question of forging and perfect workmanship are as fine as anything one can desire, and as good as one could wish for, quâ weapon. I was glad to see that the Emperor was having one of his Sadamune blades, that belonged to the Emperor Gotoba, mounted by Natsuo and another chaser, to be worn on ceremonial occasions; and also that he was having a gold lacquer book stand made, with a view of showing that the art is by no means lost, it is only the patrons that have disappeared. Judging from their cloisonné and silver work, I believe that, if fairly dealt with, the Japanese metal workers can supply art metal work and jewelry—independent of stones, of course—equal to, if not superior to, the best western work, and less commonplace and conventional. From what I have seen of their silver work, I believe them to be as great masters of the hammer as our old goldsmiths were; and our workmen of to-day are not encouraged to acquire the skill. It is rare even to come across a piece of silver thoroughly hammered—the die, the swage, and the press are more in demand than the hand of the skilled workman, and he has no chance, even if he has the tendency, either to become an artist or to know even what is or is not artistic."

On the variety of the points yet to be discussed, he wrote in his letter of the thirteenth of last month: "In fact, there is hardly a limit to what can be said about the Japanese sword as a whole. . . . No one has as yet, so far as my knowledge extends, dealt with the '*hi*,' the grooves of various forms, so admirably wrought, in the large *katana* especially, nor with the *bonji* [Sanscrit] inscriptions, or the intaglios. There are various types of the dragon, the figures of Fudô, Bishamon, Marishiten, Jurojin, Batô, Kwannon, etc., all having, I suspect, a particular significance, and not merely ornaments."

In June, 1895, he wrote: "The deeper I go into the subject the more I find there is to learn. I think I sent you a copy of a descriptive catalogue of 169 swords which a gentleman at Tokio sent me, and for which he wanted £3,000. He said he had been collecting them for sixteen years and wished to sell them as a collection. He must have been dismally imposed upon by the men he took for experts, I imagine, if I may judge by the astounding blunders after sixteen years of collecting; for they were so ludicrous that I sent him a long sheet of corrections, urging him to cancel his catalogue and reprint it, or there was no chance of his getting an offer for the collection from any one with any knowledge of swords. One of the swords is described as having one side of the blade tempered by one smith, and the other side by another. I told him that, if he had any evidence establishing the truth of that, he would get a long price for the weapon, for it would be unique. I have no reply yet."

Of the interest, depth, and importance of the subject he wrote, December 11th, 1893: "The true account of the make of blades rendered all my illustrated Japanese works on swords much more interesting and valuable, and taught me what to look for. Not that I attach the slightest value to the opinion of any expert, Japanese or other, as to the authenticity of the signature on a blade; but the details given in those works are of the greatest interest to any one conversant with arms and their manufacture. To be able to certify the maker of a Japanese blade requires not only very varied knowledge, but long practice and experience. It is as difficult as to assign a painting to its author; but to know whether one has a remarkable piece of forging, tempering,

and grinding before one is within the capacity of every lover and
student of swords. I have been that for about sixty years, and
can fully understand why the wealthy *samurai* or *daimio*, instead
of growing Cellinis to make plate and jewels for him, patronized
and protected the Gotós, the Umetadas, the Yasuchikas, the
Toshinagas, and the host of other exquisite chasers, who decorated his invaluable blades with metal work that has never been
surpassed in quality, nor equalled even in the sense of mere
working in metal. It has been a great pride and pleasure to
me to see that Tiffany at once saw what a field of artistic beauty
in metal work was opened up by these Japanese chasers. Our
manufacturers and workmen get out of old ruts with difficulty,
and our public is just beginning to have a vague idea that Birmingham and Sheffield have something to learn from Japan, a
dictum which is redolent of flat heresy to 999 of my countrymen
out of every 1,000."

In August, 1896, he says: "The number of those who take an
intelligent interest in Japanese work steadily increases, and a
wider perception spreads of the use that can be made of it in the
arts generally. Much is to be learned from it, especially as regards decorative art and metal working."

Mr. J. T. Morris spoke of the Japanese bow, and a small bronze figure with a bow, modern work, obtained at Yokohama; and exhibited a Japanese bow over seven feet long; and illustrated the subject with three Japanese books, showing in pictures the manner of holding the bow and arrow and the string, and the method of arrow release. Mr. Morris pointed out that the very long bow was held far below the middle; and that often after the discharge of the arrow the bow was whirled half round a longitudinal vertical axis, bringing the string upon the outer side of the arm. He also exhibited a bow obtained by him at Delhi, India, and a sling from Cairo.

Mr. C. Stevenson said the Delhi bow was the same as the Tibetan.

President Brinton said the Delhi bow was commonly called in general the Tartar bow. He remarked that the pictures of the books exhibited, nearly all, or quite all, showed the Mongolian arrow-release, which is unknown in the Mediterranean regions and totally unknown in America. He was also not aware of any American bow where the arrow is released from the lower third of the bow; and such a bow is also unknown in Europe.

Mr. Horner said that in ancient times short bows were used in Europe; for example, the Scythian and Roman. The longest bow in history was the English six-foot bow of Agincourt and Cressy. Therefore, this evening's bow is unique as regards its length and the place of using the arrow. He remarked upon the great need there was of keeping the bowstring dry, and of the difficulty thereby added to the use of the long bow; and on the importance of the kind of wood used for so long a bow.

President Brinton said that the North American Indians used bows up nearly to seven feet in length, made of hickory, slightly curved, probably with deer-sinews for strings.

Mr. Stevenson said that the length of the bow was determined by the height of the man and the length of his arms. The bowstrings at the time of the battle of Cressy were kept dry in the quiver. The Genoese bowmen employed in that battle had had their strings wet in a storm, and so threw away their bows as useless, and were, consequently, trodden down by the English.

Mr. Horner spoke of the battle of Cressy in the same way, and of the high development of archery among the far Eastern peoples.

Mr. Morris exhibited a coin marked: "10 Dollars Pike's Peak Gold 1860—Clark Gruber."

Mr. G. Albert Lewis exhibited a coin found at Graver's Lane Station, Chestnut Hill.

Mr. Stevenson exhibited a silver seal and sealing wax holder, with a seal at each end, one in silver and the other in crystal. It had belonged to his great-grandfather, to whom it was given by a Hessian, wounded at Monmouth or Trenton.

The Auditing Committee, through Mr. C. D. Clark, reported that they had examined the Treasurer's accounts for 1895, 1896, and 1897, and had found them correct. The report was accepted.

Mr. C. E. Dana inquired why the six-pointed star was used in the United States Treasury Department, but the five-pointed star in the other Departments.

Mr. F. D. Langenheim said that the English star was six-pointed, but the French five-pointed; and suggested that, therefore, Betsy Ross, in making the first United States flag, used the French star.

Mr. Lewis said that it was a mere myth that Betsy Ross designed the flag; that it was designed by the grandfather of Dr. Ray Barton, and that the mullet with five points was used because it occurred in George Washington's coat of arms.

APRIL 7TH, 1898.

Dr. Max Uhle, a visitor, exhibited a curious, unique, probably prehistoric implement (Fig. 5) obtained by him on an island of

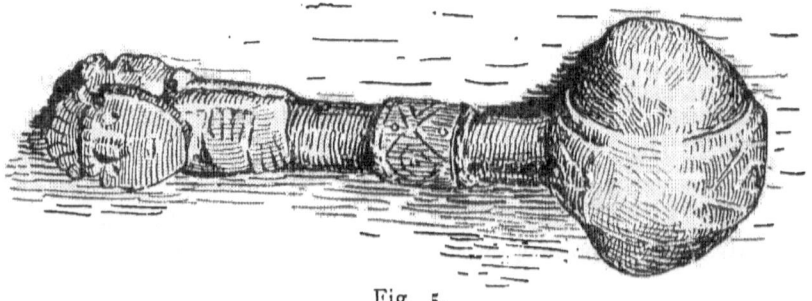

Fig. 5.

Lake Titicaca, in upper Bolivia. It was wholly of copper in the form of a hammer with a handle five and a half inches long, and a double head, about two inches long and an inch and a half in diameter, the whole imitating the form of prehistoric stone hammers that have a wooden handle bound to a stone head grooved around the middle. The faces of the copper hammer had apparently been pointed, conical; but in use had become nearly flat. The handle was elaborately ornamental in shape, especially at the outer end. Such prehistoric stone hammers are not rare in Bolivia, and he had himself found 200, being the first systematic explorer of such objects there; and there are, perhaps, 150 or 200 specimens of such hammers from Bolivia in our museums. The stone hammers are made of soft stone and other stones; and he exhibited two specimens and also drawings showing how the wooden handle was bound upon the stone head.

He also exhibited a couple of specimens of the "bola," each made of three cords, in one specimen about eighteen inches long, and in the other about four feet long, united at one end in a knot, and bearing at the other end a weight. In the larger specimen, the weights were stones of a couple of inches in diameter, enclosed in leather. In the smaller specimen, the weights were partially rounded cylindrical blocks of a light kind of wood, of about the same size. The implement is swung round the head like a sling, and thrown, and is a very effective weapon. It is also used for handling the vicuñas and for catching horses, and in that case the weights are of wood. Many of the grooved hammer stones may have been used for bolas, and examples are figured from Patagonia and Chile. Therefore, some of the Bolivian grooved stones were probably used for bolas. Some such stones are pointed. Nowadays, in Argentina, bolas are sometimes made with weights of lead.

It appears, then, that there are probably two kinds of grooved stones: some for bolas and others for hammers. Uncivilized peoples are very sparing in the variety of the shapes of their implements; and, for example, hammer stones not only may, but certainly have, been used as anchor stones or net sinkers, having the same type of shape. Such peoples use precisely the same form in various ways; for instance, tied to a stick for a hammer, or tied to a net for an anchor or sinker.

It is probable, therefore, that the axe-shaped object, the banner-axe, discussed by Cushing at a recent meeting of our Society, was also used in various ways and made of various sizes, not necessarily bearing in mind any religious significance; just as we use a small knife of a similar shape to a sword without thinking of any connection between them.

Dr. Uhle also exhibited a prehistoric bronze object from Bolivia, a tomahawk head, flat and thin, and somewhat of the shape of a housewife's mincemeat chopper. The blunt-edged blade, five and a half inches long, strongly curved, and perhaps an inch and a half broad, was joined by a shank of about the same breadth to a narrow straight handle or back perhaps four inches long, the whole about a quarter of an inch thick, or less, and nearly four inches broad. The material was bronze, copper with some tin, about two per cent., but not the tin percentage of European bronzes. The bronze was probably expressly alloyed, as the materials are not found naturally mixed. Tin ore is found in Bolivia and smelted; and he had seen crystals of tin-stone there as large as peas.

Mr. Morris described a stone double-pointed battle-axe, as it seemed, that he bought some years ago at St. Paul, Minn. The stone was about five inches long from point to point and about two inches in diameter at the middle, grooved around the middle, and had a light elastic wooden handle about 28 inches long. It was new, and apparently made for use as a weapon, and not as a ceremonial object.

Mr. Morris exhibited a coin of Nero. One side bore Nero's head, and the other a full-length figure of a man with a lyre.

Mr. Charles J. Cohen was elected a Resident Member of the Society.

MAY 5TH, 1898.

Mr. Chas. E. Dana made a communication on crowns, reading from his notes descriptions of several of the most noteworthy historical crowns. The Anglo-Saxon princes wore a fillet of pearls; Charlemagne's crown, formerly at Aix-la-Chapelle, afterwards at Nuremburg, and now at Vienna, is the most interesting of all. It is said to weigh fourteen pounds, and is divided into eight panels, and has twelve unpolished jewels. Each panel was described, some having only gems, some having inscriptions in Latin; on the top there is a cross; the crown has some additions later than Charlemagne. The English crown was first kept by the Templars, and was afterwards kept in the Tower. Blood's nearly successful attempt to carry off the crown from the Tower, in 1671, was spoken of. Special mention was made of the crown named after Edward the Confessor; and Queen Victoria's crown was described. Likewise, a description was given of the imperial crown with eight flowers and eight eagles; of the Iron Crown of Lombardy, containing a small band of iron, said to have been made from a nail of the Holy Cross; and of the crown of St. Stephen.

Mr. I. Horner remarked that the important, distinguishing part of the crown proper appeared to be the closing of the crown by arches over the top, not leaving it open like a coronet or circlet. A sovereign prince (in England, only the Queen and the Prince of Wales) has the surmounting arches as the characteristic of a monarch who has no feudal superior. Among the ancient Romans, crowns were only ornaments. As royal emblems they began to be used in the middle ages.

Mr. Dana said that the best authority as to the forms of crowns was the seals. The upper edge of the circlet of the crown of Edward I, of England, bore projections in the form of a trefoil. Edward III was the first to add the cross, in alternation with the trefoil. The cross was also placed at the top of the closed arches. The arches rest upon the crosses of the circlet, not upon the fleurs-de-lis.

Mr. Horner said he thought the crown was derived from a hat, and that it came from the East; but that the coronet or fillet was derived from a wreath.

President Brinton said that the Visigothic crosses of Spain, preserved at Toledo, date from the fifth, sixth, and eighth centuries, and are very rude. The Iron Crown, or Crown of Monza, in Lombardy, said to date from the time of Queen Theodelinda, in the seventh century, did not look to him, when he saw it, anything like so old. The story seemed to him to be folk-lore rather than history, and the crown he thought to be late mediæval.

Mr. Horner spoke of having seen American Indians in Buffalo Bill's show to-day, and said he was convinced by their physiognomy that they were of Asiatic Mongolian origin.

President Brinton declared that Mr. Horner was mistaken; but that it was not a numismatic or antiquarian subject to be discussed here.

Mr. Westcott Bailey exhibited a Cuban coin, a well engraved silver dollar, marked, " Rep. of Cuba, 1897. Patria y Libertad. Souvenir."

Mr. Richard Wistar Davids and Mr. John F. Lewis were elected Resident Members of the Society.

October 6th, 1898.

The death was announced of Rt. Rev. Wm. Stevens Perry, Honorary Vice-President of the Society, for the State of Iowa, May 10th, 1898; of Hon. Thomas F. Bayard, Honorary Vice-President for the State of Delaware, September 28th, 1898; and of Theodor M. Roest, of Leyden, Holland, a Corresponding Member, September 2d, 1898.

A bronze medal of Blumenbach was received as a gift from Mrs. Harrison Allen; and a special vote of thanks was passed.

Mr. F. D. Langenheim presented to the society the medal of the Reading Sesqui-centennial.

Mr. Culin spoke of the European museums he had visited during the past summer, with special reference to their collections of American archæology and ethnology. He described the bow and the feather-robe in the Musée de la Porte de Hal, in Brussels, attributed to the Emperor Montezuma; and the so-called bow of Montezuma in the Royal Museum of Historical Art, in Vienna. He pointed out that the bow and robe were wrongly attributed, and that they probably came from the Tupi Indians of Brazil. He spoke of the wholly inadequate manner in which America is represented in European museums, outside of Berlin; and of the obligations resting upon American institutions to collect and preserve the antiquities of this country. He exhibited photographs of the interiors of a number of the museums referred to.

President Brinton, in comment, said that there were, no doubt, many collections of American objects in Europe outside the great and well-known collections which would well repay inspection by an interested traveler. He instanced the collections of Peruvian objects in the municipal museum of the city of Cologne, collected by Dr. Constanz, whose publications had been overlooked by Mr. Dorsey; as well as the Northwest Coast collection at Boulogne-sur-mer, which that unusually acute scholar, Alphonse Pinart, had given to his native city. Central American collections are to be found in Basel. In Bremen, the municipal museum contains Costa Rican collections worthy of study. He also understood there were collections at Dieppe.

Mr. Marshall H. Saville, Curator of Archæology in the American Museum of Natural History, New York, a visitor, said he had, three years ago, made a trip through the museums of Europe similar to that of Mr. Culin. Like him, he had been impressed with the cases used in Dresden. Mr. Chas. H. Read, in London, illustrated the practical advantage of iron cases over wooden ones. An iron case that had not been opened for years had admitted practically no dust; but the interior of a wooden case needs to be cleaned after six months. In Liverpool, Mr. Saville had unearthed the Fejervary Codex, one of the most important Mexican codices, in a damp case in a basement. Through his efforts it was carefully looked after. He believed it was presented to Oxford when it was transferred from Liverpool. Two of the most beautiful specimens of feather mosaic exist in Bologna.

The Curator of Numismatics, Mr. Langenheim, reported that he had inquired of the Swedish Royal Mint whether the dies of the medal of Mr. Mickley, the first President of the Society, were still in existence. It was answered that the mint had no knowledge of their whereabouts.

Mr. Inman Horner, the Historiographer, read obituary notices of the following deceased members of the Society: Thomas Hockley, Lewis A. Scott, W. S. W. Ruschenberger, Robert H. Lamborn, J. Sergeant Price, as follows:

NECROLOGY.

BY THE HISTORIOGRAPHER OF THE SOCIETY, INMAN HORNER.

THOMAS HOCKLEY, Treasurer of our Society from the year 1888 until his death, early in 1892. He was born in Philadelphia on January 26th, 1839, his father being John Hockley, for many years the cashier of the Bank of North America, and his mother Miss Katherine Stevenson. He entered the Sophomore Class of the University of Pennsylvania, and graduated in 1859. In 1862 he was admitted to the bar of Philadelphia County, having had Charles E. Lex for his preceptor. He enlisted as a private in the Independent Artillery Company, Pennsylvania Militia, in both 1862 and 1863, when the State was invaded. In the year 1871, he married Miss Amelia Daniel, of Boston, Mass.; and he had two children, both now deceased.

Mr. Hockley was much interested in the advancement of the interests of science in his native town, and gave freely of time and labor to them. As I have stated, he was Treasurer of our Society. He was also Treasurer of the Department of Archæology and Paleontology of the University of Pennsylvania, Secretary of the Zoölogical Society, and a Trustee of the Fairmount Park Art Association—honorable, but unpaid positions. He had an extensive private collection of mediæval furnishings and archæological objects in his own home; and his knowledge of art was placed freely at the service of the Society. He passed away suddenly on March 12th, 1892, at the comparatively early age of fifty-three.

LEWIS ALLAIRE SCOTT was born in Philadelphia on August 10th, 1819, and was the son of John Morin Scott, a distinguished lawyer, and Mary Emlen, his wife, of the well-known family of that name. He was a pupil of the famous Scotch schoolmaster, Samuel Crawford, and was, no doubt, well grounded in the classics, and perhaps in little else (for that is still the way of Scotch schoolmasters) when, in 1834, he entered the class of 1838 at the University of Pennsylvania, to graduate first honor man and valedictorian of the class. He then became a civil engineer, and took part in the survey of the Philadelphia & Erie Railroad. Abandoning this, he adopted his father's profession, and was admitted to the bar in September, 1841. His practice was chiefly in the law of Real Estate. After 1864, he retired from the active pursuit of his profession. During the war, being at about the military age limit, he became an officer of the Home Guards, and attained the rank of Major.

Mr. Scott was much interested in linguistics. He devoted much time to the study of the Arabic and Syriac languages, and was an expert Egyptologist. He was a life-member of our Society, and for many years one of its Vice-Presidents. He took much interest in our discussions; and, until ill health prevented, was always present at our meetings; and all the projects for advancing the aims of the Society met his hearty and generous support. Personally, as most of us remember, he was exceedingly gentle and kindly in manner, and given to hospitality, and when ill health darkened his later years no one had more of our sympathy.

He married, in 1857, a daughter of the late Richard Wistar, and died in August, 1896, leaving a widow, three sons, and a daughter.

Dr. William Samuel Waithman Ruschenberger was born near Bridgeton, N. J., on September 4th, 1807. At the age of 20 he was appointed "Surgeon's Mate" in the United States Navy. His first service was with the Pacific Squadron, and after his return he entered the University of Pennsylvania, receiving the degree of M. D. in March, 1830. The following year he was commissioned a Surgeon in the United States Navy, and during the years 1836-39 visited the far East as Fleet Surgeon of our squadron in the Pacific Ocean. From 1854 to 1857 he was again in the Pacific Ocean. During the Civil War he was President of the Examining Board of Surgeons; and his last active service was the charge of the Naval Hospital in Philadelphia in 1873. He was retired with the title of Medical Director and the rank of Commodore, in 1874, and was for many years at the head of the list of medical officers of the United States Navy.

He died March 24th, 1894, having been for sixty-eight years in the service of the Government. He married, in 1839, Miss Mary B. Wister, and left one child, Lieutenant C. W. Ruschenberger, U. S. N. He published, in 1838, *A Voyage Around the World;* in 1854, *Notes and Commentaries During Voyages to Brazil and China*, and many pamphlets and monographs on special subjects. He naturally was a member of many learned societies, and took an active part in the meetings of all of them; especially in the American Philosophical Society, of which he was Vice-President from 1885 to the time of his death; and of the Academy of Natural Sciences, of which he was President from 1869 to 1881. He was Vice-President of the Numismatic and Antiquarian Society for many years.

ROBERT H. LAMBORN was born at Kennett Square, Chester County, Pennsylvania, in the year 1836. At an early age he entered the service of the Pennsylvania Railroad Company as assistant surveyor, or rodman; but soon after attaining his majority he went to Freiberg, in Saxony, to study metallurgy. After graduating there, he was entered as a student at the Ecole des Mines, in Paris. He also obtained the degree of Ph. D. from the University of Goettingen.

His technical knowledge of metallurgy obtained for him, soon after his return to this country, the then novel employment of Inspector of Rails for the Pennsylvania Railroad Company, a position which the increased scientific knowledge of iron and steel made useful and necessary. About the year 1866 the Pennsylvania Steel Company was formed to manufacture steel by the almost untried processes patented by Sir Henry Bessemer, and Lamborn was chosen Secretary. This company was the second formed in the United States, the first being at Troy, N. Y., under the direction of Mr. Holley. Lamborn was shortly after made Secretary of a company formed to build a railroad from the head of navigation on the Mississippi River to the head of Lake Superior, now the St. Paul & Duluth. These positions occupied his attention for many years. Later, he became interested in railroads further west, and passed much of his time in England in negotiating bonds and in charge of other important transactions involving the investment of capital.

In the meantime his own private fortune was increasing rapidly, and about 1890 he retired from business life with ample means. He began a systematic collection of pictures in Mexico, buying at liberal prices the altar pieces and such other pictures as would best illustrate Spanish art in the New World. He endeavored, too, to solve the mosquito problem, and seemed at length to have persuaded himself that the artificial cultivation of the dragon fly, commonly called the devil's darning needle, would make the extermination of the unpleasant mosquito all but certain.

I made his acquaintance in the year 1868, when he had charge of an expedition, as it might truly be called, from St. Paul to Duluth, of high railroad officials and their wives. We traveled as a caravan, carrying our own supplies over the one hundred and fifty miles, with Lamborn as master of transport; and the care and thoroughness of his manner made a deep impression on me. I recall that on the journey he pointed out to us from the car window a small farm in Iowa as the place he was in treaty to purchase, to begin life as a Western farmer, when a severe illness intervened. He was much interested in our Society and a constant attendant at our meetings.

The last time I saw him was in the autumn of 1895, at a bicycle school, where he was taking lessons in the art of bicycle riding with almost the same vigor I had witnessed thirty years before in the delicate art of managing a company of exacting tourists. He had changed but little in appearance, the same well-cared-for brown beard and wavy hair and well set up, stocky figure, a little larger in girth and the resolute eyes as bright as ever. Very soon after, we heard of his death, alone and without warning, in the hotel in New York where he passed his winters. This was the 14th day of January, 1895, in his fifty-ninth year.

JOHN SERGEANT PRICE was born in Philadelphia, June 10th, 1831, the son of Eli K. Price, who was for many years the honored President of this Society. Most of us here recall the venerable President, who, at his great age, never failed to preside at our meetings, whether the night was fine or storming, and to whose labors and countenance the Society owed much in its earlier and struggling years. The son followed in the footsteps of the father in this as well as many other directions. Although a busy man, he always found time to be at our meetings, to act on any committee, and to advance our interests in any way possible to him. His father, as all who know of business in the city of Philadelphia, was, perhaps, the ablest real estate lawyer of his time, and as a counsellor, trustee, or executor had the direction or management of estates for many owners and of many millions of dollars in value. In this he associated with him his son, John Sergeant, named after the most highly esteemed member of the Philadelphia bar; and, as the weight of years increased, the son became more and more busily engaged, until the whole of the vast business interests devolved on him. They were all managed with skill, prudence, and capacity, and the third generation of the family still keep in their hands the management of estates which the ability and fidelity of their forbears caused to be entrusted to them. Mr. Price filled many positions of trust and honor. He was for many years the Treasurer of the American Philosophical Society, a Trustee of the Western Saving Fund, and Director in a number of stock companies.

He enjoyed good health up to a short time before his death. He then suffered from a serious illness; but seemed to have recovered completely, when, on August 16th, 1897, a sudden attack of heart disease brought his useful life to a close.

President Brinton spoke on the "Archæology of the Island of Cuba."

Mr. Charles E. Dana exhibited a collection of casts of royal and other seals obtained by him at Paris.

Mr. Carl Edelheim exhibited several antique rings, including a Gothic bishop's ring.

Mr. Cornelius Stevenson exhibited a pair of fire-gilt stirrups which had belonged to General Kleber.

Mr. Culin exhibited a set of four stone dice, *u-lu lu-lu*, made of pumice stone by natives of the Hawaiian Islands, now in Philadelphia.* The dice were marked on one side with a cross, and, respectively, with one, two, three, and four dots. The opposite sides are plain. They bear a general resemblance to the bone dice used by the Indians on the eastern coast of North America.

Mr. Culin exhibited a collection of old German playing cards, purchased by him during the past summer in Nuremberg.

---

* See Hawaiian Games, *American Anthropologist*, New Series, Vol. I, p. 201.

Among them there was a pack of 32 cards, with brass backs, and with the faces covered with horn, and the four suits indicated by the colors red, green, white, and yellow. Each suit has four numbers, seven to ten, marked by Roman numerals in a wreath of green leaves; and three court cards: a grotesque man, a flower, and a crown (the king). Mr. Edelheim said that these cards were anciently used in beer shops. There were also six cards and two fragments of Nuremberg cards of the sixteenth century (assigned by Bierdimfl to 1583). There was also a pack of Nuremberg cards with sentimental and humorous copper-plate engravings and verses of the early part of the present century.

Mr. W. H. Pfahler, of 127 North Thirty-third Street, Philadelphia, was elected a Resident Member of the Society.

DECEMBER 1ST, 1898.

Professor Maxwell Sommerville read a paper on "Some Evidences of Superstition from the Desert of Sahara," and exhibited a collection of charms and amulets brought by him from the desert.

Mr. Inman Horner exhibited an ivory carving recently presented to him by Dr. J. Donaldson Smith. It was in the form of a three-clawed Chinese dragon.

Mr. Culin exhibited a number of fans recently acquired as a gift by the Museum of the University of Pennsylvania from Mrs. Joseph Drexel. Two of the fans were made for the Queen's Jubilee; one of them had a painting on gauze signed Bellini, with a Brussels lace coach inserted, with a Brussels lace border and mother-of-pearl sticks inlaid with violets in pearl and gold; and the other had Wedgewood designs in green silk, three plaques ornamented with spangles, and had enamelled and spangled pearl sticks. This last was a reproduction of one of the fans in the prize case.

The committee on nomination of officers of the Society for the coming year reported a list of names, and the whole list was unanimously elected. (See page 12.)

INDEX.

www.ingramcontent.com/pod-product-compliance
Lightning Source LLC
Chambersburg PA
CBHW031105020726
47495CB00007B/2057